DECKER'S DILEMMA

CHANTAL FERNANDO

carina
press

**carina
press®**

Recycling programs
for this product may
not exist in your area.

ISBN-13: 978-1-335-52999-2

Decker's Dilemma

Carina Press
22 Adelaide St. West, 41st Floor
Toronto, Ontario M5H 4E3, Canada
www.CarinaPress.com

Printed in U.S.A.

For Mila Chantal.
I adore you, little beauty.

DECKER'S DILEMMA

"Isn't it pretty to think so."

—Ernest Hemingway

Chapter One

Decker

"Why do you always close your curtains whenever I come over?" I cross my arms over my chest and study my baby sister, Simone.

She turns back from fixing the material and plays dumb, twiddling her blond, curly hair around her finger with wide eyes. "I have no idea what you're talking about. It's just sunny out there, and I'm trying to make sure that we don't get skin cancer," she says, blue eyes unflinching.

"I know that your neighbor grows marijuana plants, Sim. And probably more than she is allowed. I wasn't born yesterday."

She purses her lips. "I'm not confirming anything. But if she did, I don't want her to get into trouble. She's a sweet old lady and I'm sure it's medicinal."

I lean my elbows down on her kitchen countertop. "You really think I'd come to visit my sister and arrest some grandma while I'm at it?"

She shrugs. "I don't know. I just didn't want to put you in that position."

"Well, now you don't have to," I say as I move to the window and spread the curtains open, giving me full view of Mrs. Masey's giant plants. "I quit the police force."

"You did what?" Sim asks, stilling. Her brow furrows. "You aren't going to start stripping again, are you? That was awful."

I laugh out loud at that memory. "No, I'm not. Although I still have the body for it," I say as I tap my abs. I used to do a little stripping to make some extra money while I was in the police academy. No one else knows about it, at least I hope they don't.

She throws a tea towel at me. "Seriously, Seth, what are you doing?"

"I've gone to work at Nadia's firm," I explain. "As a private investigator. It gives me a little more control over what I want and don't want to do, and I'm basically working for myself. I thought it would be a nice change."

What I don't admit to my sister is that the line between what the law is and what is right has gotten a little blurred for me. It all came to a head when Nadia was hired to investigate a murder, and together we uncovered that the wrong man had been arrested and convicted. I was reprimanded for helping her and working with the Knights of Fury MC, and my boss told me I would not likely see the promotion I thought I was going to be getting. And after all of that, the fucked up thing is that I was punished for helping find justice for the victim. If Nadia asked me for help again, I wouldn't have been able to say no. I felt a little frustrated, like my skills weren't being used to the best of their ability.

And if I'm being honest, maybe being a cop wasn't all that I thought it was going to be. I wanted adrenaline, excitement and to help people while getting that rush, but all I got was rules and regulations.

Besides, I don't feel that I was making a difference as a police officer. Not as much as I would have liked. I knew it was time for a change. Maybe I'll regret my choice. Maybe not.

I don't know.

But we will soon find out.

"Private investigation. Isn't that basically the same thing without the badge?"

"Eh. More freedom, fewer rules."

"But you loved putting away the bad guys. You can't do that as a PI."

"Not true. I may not be able to physically put the handcuffs on someone, but I can still help put them away. And I can also help catch the people who aren't necessarily criminals, but are doing something wrong, and that matters more to me."

Sim sits on her countertop, legs swinging, as she gives me an inquisitive look. "I promise I'm not being negative, but don't PIs just catch cheating spouses?"

"You know, that's exactly what I thought when I first met Nadia." I smile at the memory. She had come storming into the station like she owned the place, asking my former partner, Felix, an old friend of hers, for some help on a missing persons case. Felix introduced the two of us, and I made a crack about how it couldn't be hard to find out which hotel a cheating husband was at. Nadia shook my hand, her hold strong, while staring me dead in the eye and proceeded to tell me that she was looking for a missing teenager because the cops had given up looking. Her confidence and work ethic made me respect her instantly. "But there's a little more to it than that. And I can choose the cases that I want to take on."

Sim studies me. "It must have been hard, though, for you to walk away from a job you've given your life to."

I nod slowly. "It was."

But I guess I was given a push. If they hadn't caught me helping Nadia would I have stayed? I'm not sure what my answer would be. But my actions have led me here, and I don't have any regrets.

Yet.

"As long as you're happy."

"I think it's the right choice for me. At least for now," I say, glancing around her black-and-white tiled kitchen. "And Nadia needed someone to help her out, so here I am."

Stepmom life had come a-calling. Nadia went from being a workaholic to being a woman with a family—four children and a partner, Trade. She wanted to take a step back and have a better work-life balance, so when she asked my opinion on taking someone else on, I spontaneously suggested that I might be interested. She was surprised, and asked me a few times if I was being serious. But when I told her it actually sounded like a good idea, she offered the job to me immediately.

"So…what's the pay like?" Sim asks, arching her brow.

"Decent," I reply, realizing the reality of what I did. "I mean, it's good, it just depends how many cases I take on, which is up to me. Money isn't the issue. I just needed something different. And this is a free-lance job, so I can work as many hours as I like until I figure things out."

I even spoke to Nadia about us upping our prices a little so we can make a higher profit for us both. Nadia is very modest and humble. I'd be charging much more for our services, depending on each case, of course. I'd also be willing to help people out if they needed it, don't get me wrong, but rich people can afford to pay a little more for our services.

"Okay. You are a hard worker, Seth. She's lucky to have you."

"Thanks."

"But you know, if it doesn't work out and you ever need another job, let me know," she teases, smirking as she gets down from the counter, opens the fridge, and scans its contents.

"Thanks, but no thanks." Somehow I can't picture myself grooming dogs with her at her business.

She laughs. "Come on, let's celebrate your new job then. Is it too early for cocktails?" she asks as she opens a bottle of vodka.

I glance at my watch. "Nope."

"Wonderful."

I see Mrs. Masey in her garden from the window, so I wave at her. She spots me, her eyes wide, and then ducks, hiding herself from my view.

I sigh.

At least now no one will be scared of me because of my badge.

"So where did you say you were going? And for how long?" I ask. Sim finally had a chance to hire help at the business, and now she's going on an extended vacation.

"About three weeks. And I'm just going on a road trip. I'm heading east and I'll see where I end up!"

"Well, be sure to be safe, and check in with me every couple of days."

She rolls her eyes. "Yes, Dad."

Simone makes me a Bloody Mary and orders a pizza. We try to get together every couple of weeks, but with the recent job change, it's been a while. We sit down on the couch, talking shit, just like we normally do. We've always been pretty close, and our mom always drilled it into us that we had to look after each other.

When our mom died, all we had left was each other, since neither of us had spoken to our father after he walked out on us when I was ten. So we always make time for each other, even if it's just to check in.

"This Bloody Mary needs less blood and more Mary," I tease, barely tasting the alcohol.

She laughs. "You still have to drive out of here. I think we are too old to be getting drunk in the middle of the day, Seth."

"How responsible of you."

"Responsible is my middle name," she replies, lifting her chin. "The pizza will soak up the little alcohol in there and then you can remain being a functioning adult."

My phone rings, and Nadia's name pops up.

"Hey," I say.

"Hey, are you at the office?"

I glance over at my sister. "Nope, why?"

"We just got an email about a new case. I can't take it—it involves a little bit of travel. Can you take a look and decide if it's something you can swing?"

"Okay, will do."

Traveling doesn't sound too bad. I could use a change

of scenery. We hang up and I sign into my work email, scanning the message there.

From: Constance Wilder <cwilder892@gotmail.com>
To: Hawk's Eye Private Investigators
Subject: Find a Person

Hello, my name is Constance Wilder, and I am looking to hire a private investigator to locate my half-sister, who I just found out about. I know her birth name, birthdate, and where she used to live. She may or may not still be in the Ventura County area.

I'd appreciate your help in finding her. Please let me know if you can help me. Thank you.

Ventura County. Not exactly the holiday destination that I had in mind, but I'd still have to drive over there and stay a night at least while I investigate. Traffic in Southern California is a bitch.

I weigh what I have going on and decide getting out of town wins, no matter what case I have to work. I reply and tell her that I'm happy to help her, and ask if she can send all the information she has.

The job looks easy enough, and it gets me out of town for a few days or so, which sounds appealing after the last few jobs, which were extremely emotionally draining. I'm happy to step away from the corporate embezzling, cheating spouses and petty thefts.

I finish my cocktail with Sim, have some pizza, and then head to the office. This is another benefit of my new job: I actually like it enough that I don't mind going in on a weekend.

I don't know if it's because it's new and exciting, but I love this change, and I'm glad that I followed my gut and took a chance on this.

I'm where I'm supposed to be right now, and it's a good feeling.

My search for a Cara Wilder comes up empty. Constance's email says that Cara is Caucasian and in her midtwenties, that she heard Cara is a teacher, and that she possibly might be using her mother's last name. I search for all teachers named Cara in our surrounding towns and make a list of them. Luckily Cara isn't an overly popular name, and I narrow it down to three people. I do a social media stalk and the first one is a fifty-five-year-old truck driver, while the second is a renowned Black doctor. The third one sticks out to me, not because she's the last option, but because she's drop-dead gorgeous, with shiny long brown hair, wide brown eyes and lips many women pay for.

Her last name is different from both her biological father and mother's, but she could be married. A check with the DMV shows she has the same birthdate as Constance's sister. After further research, it looks like she might have taken her stepfather's surname.

Cara Ward.

Even though her social media is private, I learn that she's a high school teacher, and Constance was right, she lives an hour or so up north. She's been pretty close to Constance this whole time, yet they never knew about each other.

I message Nadia, telling her I'm taking that case and leaving for a night.

Chapter Two

Cara

"Miss Ward, why aren't you married?" one of my ninth graders asks me.

In front of the entire class.

After starting my career in advertising and marketing, I'd decided it wasn't for me. So I followed in my mother's footsteps and became an English teacher instead.

Right now I'm wondering if I made the right choice.

"What does that have to do with your English assignment, Amy?" I ask.

I don't really know the answer to her question. I've been dating Rhett Madden on and off for a few years now. We grew up as childhood best friends, along with our other friend Clover, and we were always told how people knew we would end up together.

It was inevitable.

Destined.

We are the love story that everyone saw coming.

Eye roll.

The truth is that we agreed we'd focus on our careers before jumping into something permanent. Rhett is a member of the Wind Dragons motorcycle club, just like my own father, and just like most of the people I love in this world. He's making his way up the ranks of the MC, and I know how important that is to him. His cut is a lot more than just a vest—it's his way of life, and it consumes most of his time. The MC is lucky to have him.

Amy shrugs, and I can only guess that she heard some sort of new rumor about me. "Nothing, I was just wondering."

"She's dating that biker dude," Sam calls out from the back of the class. He's one of my more…stubborn teenagers, and often spends his days in the principal's office.

Biker dude. How simple they make Rhett sound, when he is anything but.

"There's no rulebook to when someone gets married, if ever," I tell the class. "And that's all we will be saying about that."

"Maybe she doesn't want to get married. My dad said it was the worst mistake he ever made," Peter, another student, comments.

I think about the marriage my mother has with my father. And then I think about Clover and her husband, Felix. Marriage can be a beautiful thing, as long as you choose the right person. Who you marry is a lot more important than when you get married.

I change the subject and continue with my lesson. Thank God this school year is almost over.

When the school day is finished, I get into the black Mercedes Benz CLK that my parents bought me, place all my documents on the passenger seat and head home.

I turn the music off, just because after a day of teaching, I need a little silence to process the day.

When I pull up at my big black electric gate, I press the button on my set of keys and it starts to open. Being the daughter of a biker has always made me be overly careful with security, because I have seen too many things throughout my life for me to get comfortable. I head up my driveway and wait until the gates close and lock before I get out of my car and go inside. I bought this house last year with Rhett—a newly built four-bedroom, two-bathroom, two-story home. It's close to work, and a twenty-minute drive to my parents' house and the clubhouse. This house is the one I intend to live in forever.

I feel at peace as I step inside, canvas prints covering the cream walls of the entry. I smile at the big picture of me and Clover. We're back to back and posing at a festival, both of us covered in glitter and sparkles. When Clover got married, I worried that maybe our friendship wouldn't be the same, but instead of losing my best friend, I gained another. Felix always makes me feel welcome, and lets me know how important I am in not only Clover's life, but now his, too.

Some bonds never break—they strengthen.

I get comfortable on the couch, kick off my heeled sandals and lie back with my phone in my hands. I send Rhett a message asking if he's still coming home instead of staying at the clubhouse, and then pull out the English papers that need to be graded tonight.

It's late by the time I'm done, so I order in some dinner, take a shower, and then jump into bed, getting prepared to do it all again tomorrow.

And Rhett?

He never even texted me back, and he never came home.

Just another day in the life of an almost old lady.

Friday night comes around and I meet Clover at Riley's, our local bar, to catch up. She works for the FBI but is currently taking time off so she can stay at home with her beautiful one-year-old, Sapphire, who is also my goddaughter.

"Look at this picture I took of Fire today." She beams, passing me her phone.

I smile at her big blue eyes, mop of dark hair and her mom's smile. "She is so cute."

I scroll through pictures of Sapphire with Felix, already knowing how much she has him wrapped around her finger, along with Clover's parents, Faye and Dex Black. The genes in that family are fierce, and Sapphire shares her mother's hair and eyes, so I know she'll be a knockout when she's older.

"She's trouble," Clover replies, but with pride in her tone.

"Wonder where she got that from?" I tease, swallowing the last of my beer. "It's in the bloodline."

"Her dad is normal." She smirks, referring to her cop husband, Felix. "But you're right, I have no chance—she's going to be a little hellraiser."

I'm sad that I don't get to see them as much lately and be part of my goddaughter's everyday life. Clover moved down south when she went to the police academy and met Felix, which is about two hours away, with traffic. I thought when she quit the force she'd move back, but she and Felix made a home down there, so I only see them every few months.

"There's a reason that Fire is the perfect nickname for her." I grin.

Clover puts her phone away and studies me, before moving her eyes to her drink and twirling her straw around the vodka. "So how's things with Rhett?"

Here we go. You'd think that she'd let me finish my drink first before going for the jugular.

"Good," I say after a little hesitation. "He's been busy with the MC. You know how it is."

"But I mean, he's coming home every night, right?" she asks, still focused on her beverage, unable to look at me. "And you two are happy?"

I purse my lips and realize there is no point in lying to her. "No, he's not home a lot, to be honest with you. He stays at the clubhouse a fair bit."

It's embarrassing to admit, even to my best friend who was born into this life and would understand more than anyone. Rhett used to come home late, but he'd still come home. Now not so much. He says that it's just easier to stay there.

She stirs her straw a few more times. "I'm going to say something and it's something I've never said before to you, but before I do, I want you to give me the benefit of the doubt and remember that killing me will leave your goddaughter motherless."

I stick out my tongue at her. "Yeah, yeah, go on. Say what you want."

She takes a deep breath. "The MC will always come first to him, but that means you will always come in

second. Do you think that you will be okay with that?
For the rest of your life?"

My eyes widen, not expecting her to ask that. She,
like me, grew up in this world. It's all that we have ever
known. Love the man, love the club. "I knew what I
was getting into."

"That's not what I asked. Cara, it's me. And you
know I'm always going to be honest with you. I just
want to make sure that you are happy."

Happy.

"I've seen how you are with Fire—you're going to
be a wonderful mother someday. Have you and Rhett
spoken about starting a family?" she presses when I
stay silent, still pondering her words. "Or maybe getting married at some point?"

We did, when we were younger, but haven't in a while.

Happy.

I'm still stuck on that word.

Am I happy?

"I love Rhett," I manage to say. "I don't know. My
mom always stood by Dad even when it got hard."

"So you feel like you have to do the same with
Rhett?" Clover finishes, frowning.

"No. Yes. I don't know. We grew up in this life, Clo.
We've seen our mothers sacrifice for our fathers." Rhett
and Cara. Cara and Rhett. It's what is supposed to be.

Clover turns to me, giving me the full Black-Banks
stare. "Yes, our mothers sacrificed for our fathers. But
that was their choice. They love them and knew that
deep down our fathers would always put them first.
They'd never put the club before them. You know that.
I know that. Everyone knows that."

I open my mouth to argue, but realize I don't have anything to say. She's right. No matter how much my father loved the Wind Dragons, my mother, my sister, and I always came first.

When she reads the realization on my face, she gives me a sad smile. "You don't have to stay with Rhett because everyone thinks you're destined, Cara. Being destined doesn't mean he can take you for granted. And no one will feel like you failed if you chose a different path. I chose a different path."

I sigh heavily. "I texted him to see if he was coming home last night. He didn't, and never even replied. He called me earlier today and said he was busy with club shit."

"Yeah, I hear they've been keeping him pretty busy," she agrees, taking a sip of her drink and then putting it back down again. "You know I love Rhett. Hell, I would take a bullet for him. But I will not sit here and watch you waste away your life because of some image you had when you were sixteen! Is this the life you envisioned? Or better yet, is this the life you wanted?"

Her words reach a part of me that I've been burying. Realizing how long I've just been going through the motions, pretending that everything is fine.

Am I fine?

I don't want to lose Rhett. He's a part of me, and he's been in my life since I can remember. He's one of my best friends. But did we get it all wrong? What if that's all we were meant to be?

Friends.

"Where is all of this coming from?" I ask. "You've always said that Rhett and I were meant to be together."

"Maybe I was wrong," she admits, showing me a picture on her phone. "Look at you here. Look at your smile. I haven't seen that smile in so long."

I stare at the picture of the three of us at our high school graduation. I can't even recognize that girl anymore.

"I smile all the time."

"It doesn't reach your eyes like it used to," she says. "I want that back for you. I want you to be happy and loved, and I think Rhett is falling short with that right now. He didn't even reply to you last night? You live together! Have we set the bar so low for men that this is suddenly okay? I would kill Felix if he did that to me without a damn good reason."

I scrub my hand down my face because she's so right. I keep making excuses for him because he's a biker and I grew up in the biker life. But Clover is accurate. My father never treated my mother this way once they committed to one another.

"I don't think this is the life I imagined," I admit to her, and to myself for the very first time. "Ideally I'd want someone who comes home to me every day, and my own family. I want to be happy and not wondering what the hell my man is doing every night."

"And you deserve all of that, Cara. That and more," she says gently. "It's not too much to ask. I feel like we all pushed you into this, saying Rhett is the one for you, and now here we are. Maybe you shouldn't listen to anything that I say from now on."

I laugh out loud. "Things change, Clo. That doesn't mean that you were wrong."

At the time Rhett and I first got together, nothing felt more right. But people change.

I know that I have.

"Speak of the devil," she mutters, eyes toward the entrance.

I know he's here without looking, I can just sense it in the air. I usually recognize the sound of his bike but mustn't have been paying attention over the music and the intense conversation.

I turn my head, and there he is.

Blue eyes.

Long blond hair.

Wind Dragons MC cut.

All the women turn to look at him, and I don't blame them. He was born for this lifestyle. I just don't know if I was.

"Hey," he murmurs, kissing the top of my head, and then doing the same to Clover. "A little birdie told me that you both were here. You look beautiful, Cara."

"Thank you," I reply, watching as he takes a seat and calls the bartender over.

"I look amazing too, you don't need to tell me," Clover comments, easing the tension. "Now tell us, Rhett, where have you been all week? I tried to call you."

"I've been busy," he replies, turning to us. "Another round?"

We both stay silent. I arch my brow. Did he really think he was going to get away with that explanation?

He sighs and runs his hand through his hair. "Some shit went down this week. I had to take care of some stuff for the Prez. I'm sorry, Cara, about last night, and I'm sorry, Clo, for not calling you back. It's been hectic."

"Is everything okay?" Clover asks, frowning.

He nods. "Yeah, it's all good now. Which is why I thought I'd come and try to make it up to you both with my presence."

"You're going to need something more valuable than that," Clover teases with a nudge.

"Haha. How's my goddaughter?" he asks Clover.

"You'd know if you came and visited," she fires back, then sighs. "She is fine."

That's another thing, Rhett and I will always be Sapphire's godparents, and even if we do ultimately split up, we'll always have that tie, on top of many others.

"I'll come and see her soon, I promise." he replies, blue eyes softening. "I said I'm sorry—how long are you both going to be mad? Come on, I'll pay for all the drinks it's going to take to make you both happy again."

"Better offer." Clover smirks.

He turns to me and cups my face. "You aren't as easily bought as Clo, are you?"

"What do you think?" I mutter, but I can feel the anger fade away. With the puppy dog eyes he gives me, it's hard to stay mad at him. But the conversation with Clover has me seeing things a little differently, and now I'm seriously confused and questioning everything. What are we doing?

I want to ask him, are we happy?

But I don't.

Instead we all have a drink together, and fall into that comfortable familiarity that we all share.

"How are those high school kids treating you? Do I need to ride into the school and scare any little punks into respecting you again?" Rhett asks, eyes full of mischief. He did that when I first started and was having some trouble with a group of senior boys. They were making inappropriate comments toward me, and I made the mistake of mentioning it to him.

"Nope, I've got it all under control, thank you," I reply in a dry tone. "How about you? Any club girls that I need to bring into line...again?"

Yeah, the man across from me makes me crazy, and not in a good way. I've acted in ways I'm embarrassed of. And I shouldn't be fighting over any man. That's not the person I want to be.

Clover downs the rest of her drink. Poor girl, always stuck in the middle.

Rhett clears his throat. "No, I don't think you need to make a scene like that ever again."

"That's dependent on your actions, not mine."

See?

Crazy.

Clover laughs under her breath. "Okay, it was a little bit funny. Cara is usually so self-contained, but in that moment even I was scared of her."

"You and me both," Rhett replies.

Now it's my turn to down my drink.

"Are we still going away next month or has that changed?" Clover asks us, referring to the road trip we had planned for the long weekend. "We need to decide now so I can book the accommodations."

"I'm in," I reply, looking forward to the beach getaway. "Rhett?"

"Sorry, I forgot," he replies, wincing.

Clover sighs. "What a surprise."

I'm not surprised either. We definitely aren't on his

list of priorities these days, and it hurts. We all used to be so close, and now it feels like everything is different.

"We can all go another time. It's just really hectic right now. Not that I'd ever admit it to his face, but Arrow is getting older now, and he needs my help."

"Yeah, yeah," Clover replies, but still sounds disappointed.

I know how she feels.

Two beautiful women saunter up to the bar, right next to us, both checking out Rhett. Yes, he's a good-looking man, but it's the cut that really draws their attention, and I know that because it happens no matter which biker I'm around at the time.

Hell, it still happens when I'm out with my dad, and he's in his fifties.

I asked my mom once how she deals with it, and she shrugged and said, "He's mine. He goes home with me, and he's not going to give them the time of day. I have nothing to worry about."

One of the women smiles and winks at Rhett, and he turns, finding me watching him. He wraps his arm around me and kisses my temple. "I really am sorry, Cara. I know I haven't been around. But I'm going to make it up to you tonight."

I soften as he presses his lips against mine, and then against my forehead. He gazes into my eyes and I remember why I fell in love with him, but when he looks away, the connection fades and reality sets back in once again.

Relationships aren't always easy. Maybe this is just a phase, a rut that we are stuck in. Sure, he's been busy recently, but we have a life together.

And it's not all bad. Rhett and I know each other so well, and we have a connection that isn't so easy to give up on.

I know how he's going to make it up to me tonight.

But for the first time ever, I question if it's going to be enough.

Chapter Three

Decker

After checking into the hotel, I grab my keys and go for a drive to get something to eat and scope out the town. I know this is work, but it feels good to get away, and it's almost like a little mini vacation. Come to think of it, I can't even remember the last time I had any kind of break—it's been all work, no play for me ever since I graduated the police academy.

I end up on the beach for sunset, coffee in hand and a smile on my face as I watch the waves crash on the sand, the sun disappearing in front of my eyes. This career change for me is more than just gaining freedom—it comes with a whole new perspective on life, and a little self-care for me. I needed this.

"Hey," a pretty redhead says to me, waving as she approaches. She's wearing a green bikini, her lips painted in gloss. "You here alone?"

"Pretty sure that's supposed to be my line," I tease. She takes that as an invitation and sits down next to me.

Getting women has never been an issue for me. Finding one that I can really, truly connect with and want to stick around? Whole different issue. I know how I come off, and how people see me. A woman once told me that I'm the kind of man you enjoy but never keep. I didn't know what to think about that, but I guess she was right, because I've never been kept. They see the confidence, charm, the smile, the green eyes that can get me anything I want, and they judge me from that. But there's a lot more to me, which most people wouldn't know. I've always been a jokester, but underneath I'm a deep thinker, and I like to relate to other people on that level.

"Equality," she replies, nodding toward the water. "Want to take a dip?"

I shake my head. "I have to get back to work. Thanks for the offer, though."

I walk back to my car and drive back to the hotel. Enough playing around. This isn't a vacation. I'm here for a reason, and her name is Cara.

It's not exactly appropriate to hang around a school, but that's where I find myself come Monday afternoon, parked just outside the gates, watching as people come in and out. I personally don't know why anyone would want to be a high school teacher, but props to them, because someone has to do it and I'm glad it's not me.

I look down at the DMV picture I have of Cara. She's an attractive woman. Extremely so. Warm brown eyes, smiling right at me, long, lush brown hair and her lips upturned at one corner. I find myself wondering how she will react to finding out that she has a half sister. Or maybe she already knows and doesn't care. Some people aren't so friendly with certain sides of their family, and the fact that she took her stepfather's last name makes me think she isn't too close with her own biological father.

She apparently has a boyfriend who is a biker; I saw his name on the deed to her house. I hope that's not going to be an issue for me and he's not going to cause any problems. I'm here today to make sure I have the right woman, and to figure out the best way for Constance to approach her.

I must admit it was a little bit of a surprise when I realized Cara knows someone I know. What do they call it? Six degrees of separation? But I should've put two and two together when I found out who her stepfather was—Adam "Rake" Ward, an infamous member of the Wind Dragons MC. My ex-partner's wife, Clover, is a "princess" of the Wind Dragons, something I gave Felix shit about when I first met him.

I saw a photo of Cara on Clover's social media and called Felix, leaving a message. I let my phone fall onto the leather of the passenger seat when I see her walking to her car. She's dressed with all class in a black blouse, tailored pants and heels. Her hair is down and reaches her waist. It's the first thing I notice about her. It's beautiful.

She drops one of the folders she's holding in her hands, mutters a curse, and picks it up, juggling her bag, phone and keys. My lips twitch. She's amusing to watch, that's for sure. "Rapstar" by Polo G plays in my car, and I mouth the words as I wait for her to get into her Mercedes Benz and drive off.

And then I follow her.

We drive for a couple of minutes and then she stops at a park, but doesn't get out of her car. She sits there and does something on her phone for a few minutes, and then gets back on the road.

Okay, that was weird. She must have just stopped to send a text or something, but she could have done that before she left the school.

Women are unusual creatures.

I stay a few cars behind her and follow her through the city. When we get to the house she owns with her boyfriend, I can tell it has high security by the electric gate out the front. No one is coming to this woman's house who isn't invited, that's for sure.

I park across the road in front of one of her neighbors' houses, hoping they aren't home, but if they are I'll just pretend I'm lost and trying to figure out directions. I like to think I'm always one step ahead, but when Cara crosses the road and comes over to my car, I have to admit that this has never happened to me before.

She knocks on my window. I roll it down, intrigued.

It's then I notice her reaching into her bag, holding something in there. "Why are you following me?" she asks, anger filling her eyes.

"I have no idea what you are talking about," I say to her, flashing her a charming smile. "I'm lost and looking for directions on how to get back to my hotel."

"I saw you at the school and then I noticed you following me to the park, and now here," she replies, pursing her lips at my answer. "I'm not stupid."

Clearly.

I've never felt so called out in all of my life. Maybe I need to rethink being a PI 'cause *stealthy* doesn't seem to describe me.

"Is that a gun in your bag?" I ask calmly. I don't

think I've ever had a woman threaten me with a gun in her handbag before, and I don't know how to feel about it.

"Who are you with?" she demands, eyes narrowing. "I'm sure you know who my dad is, and he's on his way right now, so if you don't tell me the truth, he will torture it out of you himself."

Jesus.

These biker chicks aren't messing around.

And she's a teacher?

"If you are teaching the youth of today, I'd say we're all fucked, wouldn't you?" I can't help myself from saying.

"So I was right, you were at the school!"

Oh, fuck. She played me.

"I was at the school—one of my kids goes there." I'm just talking shit at this point, because it's my only shot at not blowing my cover. Funny she brought her dad into this and not her partner, who as far as I know is also a biker.

"You said you were staying at a hotel, which means you don't live here," she points out, shaking her head. "Is anything that comes out of your mouth the truth?"

I shrug. "Sometimes." When I see her hand twitch in her bag, I realize I probably should stop joking around. "Okay, fine. I was following you. I'm looking for someone, and I think you are her. Cara Ward?"

"Who the fuck is asking?"

Wow. She's angry.

"My name is Seth Decker, and I'm a private investigator," I explain. "I have my card right here which

I can show you as proof. I'm no threat to you, I can promise you that."

"You'll have to forgive me for not blindly trusting you with that one," she murmurs, taking her hand out of the bag when her neighbor comes out.

"Cara? Are you okay?" an elderly lady calls out.

"Yes, Mrs. Treble, was just checking who was at your house. But it's just a young gentleman looking for directions."

I realize now why she came to confront me. She knew her elderly neighbor was here, most likely alone, and must have wanted to make sure nothing would happen to her.

She's a brave woman, and my respect immediately grows for her.

"I have an old map if he needs it," Mrs. Treble offers kindly.

"It's okay, he sorted it and he's about to be on his way," Cara calls back out to her.

The cute old lady waves and heads back inside. Cara ducks her head closer. "Could you please get the fuck out of here? And don't come creeping around here again."

"You aren't curious?" I ask, surprised.

"Of course I am, but I'm also not an idiot, so I'm not going to get into this right now while I'm alone."

"We could meet somewhere public and have a chat. You choose the place and time."

She studies me, eyes flashing. "Okay, but I'm bringing someone with me."

I shrug. "Doesn't bother me. Just make sure it's someone you don't mind knowing your personal business."

Her brow furrows, and I catch a glimpse of worry in her eyes.

I don't know why, but I quickly make sure she knows she has nothing to worry about. "It's nothing bad, so don't stress about it."

"Give me that card you mentioned," she demands, holding out her gun-free hand, her hair blowing behind her with the wind.

I pull one of my newly printed cards out of my glove box and hand it to her. Our fingers accidentally touch as she takes it from me and reads the card. I ignore the sparks that I felt with just a simple touch.

"Seth."

"Call me Decker."

"Decker," she corrects, studying me. "I'll meet you tomorrow. I'll message you when and where."

"Okay."

She opens her mouth, then closes it, and walks away. I watch her get back to her gate, open it and disappear inside.

She's a beautiful woman.

Fiery.

Spirited.

Why do all the bikers get the good ones?

I don't know, but I find myself looking forward to tomorrow, even though this is a complication I don't need right now. I'm attracted to someone who a) has a boyfriend and b) a client has asked me to find.

I reverse from Mrs. Treble's driveway and head back to the hotel.

Today did not go how it was supposed to, but sometimes you just have to roll with the punches.

Chapter Four

Cara

I contemplate inviting someone to join me to meet up with Decker, but I know that they would turn it into a big thing. Decker would probably end up getting a fist in his face or something dramatic because of how over-protective the men in my life are, especially my dad.

I was going to call Rhett, but I decide not to. One, be-cause I haven't heard from him since we spent the night together after he met Clo and me at the bar, and two, I know he won't take kindly to Decker following me.

I don't know what to think about the whole Decker thing. I noticed his car following me when I stopped at the park to play Pokémon Go. I recognize that it seems silly, but it's something I enjoy and share with a few of my students. I stopped to put my Gengar in the gym at the park, and noticed Decker stop, too. Growing up how I did, it's built in me to be aware of my surroundings. I'm always paying attention, always alert. I don't know if it's a good or bad thing, because I can never properly relax, but it's a skill that has kept me safe.

Last minute I end up giving Clover a call, but she

doesn't pick up, so I show up at our meeting spot, which I decided was going to be at Riley's, alone.

Decker doesn't have to know that, though. He can sit there and wonder who I'm with and who is watching me. I have a feeling that will annoy him.

I did Google him when I got home, and I found out that he was a cop in the same city as Felix. The cop thing would normally have me feeling a little suspicious, but maybe he knows Felix. I found on a website that he is now working as a private investigator for a firm down by where Clover lives, but I have no idea what he would want with me. I just hope it doesn't have anything to do with the Wind Dragons MC, and my family ties to them. I don't want to have to deal with any drama right now, but things usually have their way of finding me.

When I park my car I see him through the window, already there and waiting. At least he's prompt.

Stepping inside the bar, I find him sitting at a booth, beer in one hand, phone in the other. He's a good-looking man, this Decker, and I'm sure he's the kind of guy who knows it. He's dressed in all black: leather jacket, a T-shirt and jeans. Throw in some thick dark hair and all the darkness just makes his green eyes pop even more.

"Hey," I say, sitting down opposite him and placing my handbag down on the table.

"Hey," he replies, giving me a quick once-over. "Can I get you something to drink?"

I shake my head. "No thank you. So, you were a cop?"

He grins and arches his brow. "Looked me up?"

"Yeah. You don't have any social media, which is unusual enough, but I found an article about you online.

I thought you said you were a PI." I actually like the no social media thing, but I'm not going to admit that.

"I am. I was a cop, I quit, and now I'm a PI," he explains, shrugging. "What's the big deal—you have a warrant out for your arrest?"

"Very funny. I just want to make sure that you are who you say you are."

"I am. I think we may have someone in common."

My eyes widen in surprise. "I doubt that."

He gives me a know-it-all smirk that on anyone else would give him an "I want to punch you in the face" vibe, but instead gives him an "I want to make out with your face" look. "Clover Black."

"How do you know her?" I ask, keeping my expression neutral.

"I used to be partners on the force with her husband, Felix."

Small world indeed. "Okay, I just want to know what the hell we are doing here, and then I'll be on my merry way."

His lip twitches. "Where's your entourage?"

"Around."

He slides over a folder. "I am indeed a PI, and I was hired by a woman looking for you."

I open the file and start to read the information in front of me. It says that a woman by the name of Constance Wilder has been searching for me.

"Constance Wilder," I say, testing the name out. "We share the same biological father?"

Decker nods. "Wade Wilder."

"I haven't seen Wade since I was a kid." He never wanted anything to do with me, and to be honest, the feeling is mutual. From what I remember of him, he was not a good man. "So I have a half sister?"

"You sound surprised."

I am.

To me, Rake is my father, and I don't really think about Wade at all. Rake is the one who has been there for me and loved me as his own for as long as I can remember. With Rake as my father, I never felt like I was missing out on anything and never ever thought about reaching out to Wade or that side of the family.

"She wants to meet me?" I ask, a little curious, but also a little suspicious. If this Constance is anything like our father, maybe I don't want to know her. Hypocritical of me, I know, but I'm nothing like Wade.

Decker nods, studying me a little too closely. "She does. I can leave her information with you, and then it can be up to you what you do with it."

I arch my brow at him. "Don't you work for her?"

He laughs, and it's a deep, sexy sound. "I work for myself."

"I'd like to meet her. I mean, I'd like to hear what she has to say," I decide. I'm extremely close with my baby sister, Natalie, and I never imagined that I would have more siblings out there who want to connect with me. I should at least give Constance a chance. If she's not a good person, then I don't have to have anything to do with her. But I can at least give her that chance, right?

I just hope I don't regret it.

"Can I get you a drink now?" he asks, studying me.

"Sure, I'll have a beer, but then I better get going. I have stuff to do."

He nods and heads to the bar to buy my drink, while

I contemplate how weird my life has become. Yesterday I almost pulled an unloaded gun on him—not that he knows that—and today he's buying me a drink. He knows more about my life than I do right now, and it's messing with my head.

Constance.

In this moment I'm glad that I came here alone, because I know that no one is going to like this idea, my parents especially. Wade has always been one to use whatever and whoever he can to get what he wants— usually money, or so I've heard—and it could be that he's using his daughter to get something he wants now.

Is this a plan of theirs, or am I just jaded?

"You look worried. Is everything okay?" Decker asks, his gaze locked on me. He has beautiful green eyes, like the ocean, framed in thick dark lashes.

He slides me my beer and I expel a deep sigh. "I haven't seen my sperm donor since I was six years old, and he is a deadbeat. So just wondering what his daughter is going to be like."

His eyes widen, and he nods in understanding. "You don't have to see her if you don't want to."

"I know. I have an idea—what if I hire you to find dirt on her? Can you do that?" I ask.

"Wow, you have trust issues, don't you?"

"I'm serious."

"I could run a background check on her. What exactly am I looking for?"

"I want to know if she's genuine. If she really wants to meet me, or if she just wants something from me."

"Major trust issues," he mutters.

I ignore that. "It's not a conflict of interest?"

He laughs under his breath. "Like I said, I work for myself. I can finish my job for Constance, which I have since I've found you, and then I can start working for you."

"You switch loyalties like that all the time?" I ask, unable to stop myself.

He shakes his head. "No, when I'm loyal to someone, I'm loyal as fuck. This is business, though, and you seem like a nice woman, which I'm surprised that I'm saying considering you almost pulled a gun on me yesterday."

I flash my teeth at him. "When are you going to let that go? And I'm not one to mess with. Best that you know that now."

"I can see that."

"But neither are you," I admit. I can sense that. I've been around deadly men my entire life. A wolf can smell a wolf. And Decker is a pack leader. An alpha.

"You're smart, too," he replies, glancing away and taking a drink.

I don't know why we are sitting here, having this conversation. We just met. I don't know him, or know how trustworthy he is. Yet I find myself feeling comfortable. A little too comfortable.

"When do you head back?" I ask.

"Tomorrow. You know, it's sad, but this has been the closest thing I've had to a vacation in a long time," he admits. "And I'm not even far from home."

"That *is* sad." I grin and look down at his hand. There's no ring there, but he must have a woman to go home to.

Why am I thinking about this?

I clear my throat and look toward the stage as a band starts to play some sexy, chill jazz music. "Why did you leave the police force?"

"You still don't believe me?" he asks, amusement flashing in his gaze.

I shrug but say nothing.

"It's a long story."

He's clearly not going to give that away, and I hate that I'm curious. "You can ask me something."

He arches his brow. "Okay. Why isn't your boyfriend here keeping an eye out on you? Did you even tell him what's going on?"

I purse my lips. I don't want to talk about Rhett with him, or admit that no, I did not tell him what's going on. Shittiest Girlfriend of the Year Award goes to me. "I didn't want to worry him, so no, I did not. Your turn."

He nods slowly. "I helped a friend of mine exonerate someone who was convicted of murder, the cops found out I shared confidential information, and I was told I was not going to get my promotion. I needed a change, so I left."

"That's not what I was expecting," I admit.

So he's not here to find shit on the Wind Dragons. Good to know.

"How did you and Felix get along as partners?" I mentally tell myself to ask Felix, but I want to hear Decker's perspective. Felix is one of those straight-shooter, do-gooder type of guys who is actually very loyal and trustworthy. If Felix likes this guy, then that is saying something.

Decker smiles a megawatt smile, and I'm momentarily blinded by his good looks. *You have a boyfriend,*

Cara. "Felix is my boy. I was paired with him shortly after Clover left the force, and things were great. He is a really levelheaded guy."

We chat a little more, finish our drinks, and I throw some money on the table for mine. Decker looks at me like I've insulted him.

I grin. "What? This wasn't a date. You don't have to pay for me."

"It doesn't matter what it is. If I'm here, I'm paying," he grumbles, adding more money on top of mine just to make a statement.

I shake my head at him, amused. "Well, it was nice to meet you."

"Come on, I'll walk you to your car," he says, and we both walk out together, like it was a date. *It's not a date, Cara. You have a boyfriend.*

"Did you mean that?" he asks, as I open my car door and sit inside.

"What?"

"That it was nice to meet me?"

I close the door, turn the car on and lower my window, looking out at him. "I don't say anything I don't mean."

He smiles, and I drive off.

Chapter Five

Decker

What the fuck was that?

Sitting in my car, I try to process everything that just happened. I've never had a mark turn into a client and want information on my original client. I call Nadia and ask her if this is a thing and how ethical it is.

I can hear her amusement on the other end. "Surprisingly, no, this has never happened to me. What are you going to do?"

"What do you think I should do?"

"Decker, you make the rules. You found Cara, which is all you were asked to do. The job for Constance is done. If Cara wants to hire you, that's up to you."

"I told her that I would," I admit.

Apparently I can't say no to some pretty brown eyes and a nice smile.

A nice smile that is very taken.

By a biker.

"Well, then I guess you've found yourself your next job."

It's that easy, and that complicated.

I drive back to the hotel and close up everything for Constance's case, still thinking about Cara. I wonder when the last time was that I was so easily swayed by a woman, and can't even remember, because it's been that long.

If ever.

I go out to get something to eat when I pass a club called Rift, with loud music and lots of people standing out front, and decide to make a stop.

One more drink wouldn't hurt. I'm on vacation, after all.

When I step inside, I can see why the club is so packed. It has a really cool vibe to it, is stylishly decorated, and the DJ clearly knows what she is doing. I sit in front of the bar, order a beer and scan the dance floor.

"You following me?" a woman asks, and I turn and see the redhead from the beach.

"Small towns, right?"

She laughs. "Yep, and this is the only good place to go to on a weeknight. Every night is a Saturday night here. I'm Becca, by the way."

"Nice to meet you," I reply. "How come every time I see you, you're by yourself?"

She points over to one of the booths. "My friends are all there. Want to come and sit with us?"

"Sure." Why not?

She brings me over to a table of five beautiful women. I've had worse nights.

"Ohhh, you are sexy," one openly says to me. "Why do you always find the good ones, Becca?"

Becca smirks, seemingly loving the attention. "I have good luck, I guess."

I spend the next two hours talking shit with my new friends, and decide fuck it, I can just taxi it back to the hotel and get my car in the morning. Becca has been eying me all night—I know she wants to fuck me, and I can't think of a reason to say no. She's pretty, and I know she will be wild in bed. A man can just sense these things, and I don't miss the look in her eyes.

"You ready to go, Decker?" she whispers in my ear, and I nod.

"Yeah, let's go."

We head outside Rift, and I stop in my tracks when I see none other than Cara. She's standing on the other side of the club entrance with a man, and the two of them are yelling at each other. He's wearing a cut, so I know it must be her partner, Rhett. Biker or not, I tell Becca to stay put and walk over to Cara to make sure that she's okay. I can see that she's crying, the closer that I get.

"Why do you do this to me? We are done, Rhett. I'm so done with being second to the MC, and second to the life you want to live. Go and fuck your whores, because I am so fucking done!" she yells at him.

"Cara," he growls, grabbing her wrist as she tries to walk away.

"Cara, are you okay?" I ask, standing next to her.

"Who the fuck are you?" Rhett asks me, a muscle ticking in his jaw. Yeah, he was already angry, and now he's going to try to take that out on me. But you know what? I could take him. As long as no other MC members come and try to save his ass.

"Decker?" Cara whispers, confused to see me.

"Yeah, I'm fine. I'm just going home, like I should have from the start."

"I'll walk you to your car." Again.

"The fuck you will." Rhett seethes, trying to move Cara out the way to get to me.

"Leave him alone, Rhett," she says, standing between us, facing him. "Just go back to the woman you were here with in the first place."

Oh fuck.

Who in their right mind would cheat on a woman like Cara? I'm pissed at Rhett, for Cara and just in fucking general, because how stupid can he be?

Things are about to get real messy, and I'm about to tell him exactly what I think of him when a familiar voice says, "What the hell is going on here? Decker? What are you doing here?"

I turn around and see none other than Felix. "What are *you* doing here?"

I look next to him and see his wife, Clover, looking surprised and confused. Right, Cara and Clover know each other.

Cara runs to Clover and the two of them embrace. Felix pulls me aside. He opens his mouth, then closes it. "You know Cara?"

I shrug. "I called you, but then I got a little distracted." By Cara herself.

"That's right. My bad. I was off yesterday and today, so we came to town for her uncle's birthday party. Clover wanted to drop into Rift for old times' sake on the way there. Why are you here?"

"I'm here on a case." I decide to tell him the truth on

how I know Cara, since I was going to tell him anyway. "It has to do with Cara. Why are you here?"

"This is Clover's hometown. She and Cara are best friends. So I'm going to need to know what you want with her," he says, looking toward his wife. "Or Clover is going to kill me."

What a small fucking world.

I give him the rundown on the client who has been looking for her. I don't tell him too many details because that is Cara's information to disclose. "Okay. I get all of that. But why were you just about to get into a brawl with Rhett? That part of the job, too?"

I glance away, wincing. "I came to Rift, randomly saw Cara, and she was crying so I came to check on her. You know I'm not going to say no to a fight if one finds me."

Felix laughs and slaps me on the back. "You haven't changed at all."

"Maybe not, but from what I gathered, Rhett was here with another woman, so he deserves whatever he gets."

Felix's eyes widen. "Oh, fuck."

"Exactly."

"Come on," he murmurs, and I follow him back over to Clover. Cara and Rhett are speaking together quietly a few feet away from us.

Clover's brows rise as we approach them. "I don't think this biker bar has seen this many cops since it got raided."

I laugh. "Not a cop anymore."

"You and me both." She grins and leans in to give me a hug. "Hey, Decker."

"Do you think she will be okay?" I ask, watching Cara stand with her arms crossed and her chin tilted as Rhett tries to calm her down.

"She will," Clover assures me, nodding. Sadness flashes in her eyes. "I love Rhett, he's family to me, but I can't believe he'd disrespect and betray her like this. I'm fuming. Wait until I get him alone."

Cara comes over to us, and Rhett heads back into the club, lifting his arms behind his head in obvious frustration. Her eyes look a little red, from anger or tears I'm not sure, but she puts on a brave face.

"Come on, let's get out of here. You need a drink. Or ten," Clover says, wrapping her arm around her.

Cara sighs and nods. She then glances between us, blinking slowly. "This world is way too small."

"You're telling me."

I want to hug her, and tell her life is only going to get better for her after getting rid of the dead weight that is her, hopefully, soon to be ex-boyfriend.

She needs someone who is going to make her a wife, not a part-time girlfriend.

Becca takes the inopportune moment to come up to me and grab my arm. Felix looks on in amusement. "You're here for how long? Two nights?"

I flash him a look that begs him to shut up. Being my ex-partner, let's just say the man knows me quite well. Right now he doesn't need to be saying anything in front of Cara, because she doesn't need to know that side of me, and fuck, she just found her man with another woman. I doubt she wants another womanizer.

"Sorry, going to head off with my friends," I say to

Becca, forcing a smile and gently removing her arm. "Maybe next time."

She scowls but leaves, and I turn to find Cara's eyes on me, watching my interaction.

Dammit.

Felix looks at Clover and comments in an amused tone, "Nice to see some things never change."

"Oh, things are changing, all right," she comments, glancing at her best friend, who still has her eyes on me. Great, now she's going to think I'm some fuck boy.

Hell, maybe I am.

I don't know why I care what she thinks. I mean, she is clearly in a messy situation of her own and I don't need to be worrying about anything to do with her.

"You drove here?" Felix asks me.

I nod. "Yeah, I'll taxi it back to the hotel and come get my car in the morning."

"We'll give you a ride," he offers, nodding to his car across the road. "Do you want to come and hang out with us first? I haven't seen you in a few weeks now."

"Sounds good."

And that's how I ended up back at the Wind Dragons clubhouse.

I came here on a good night, or a bad one, depending on how you look at it. It's someone's birthday, which is why Clover and Felix came to visit in the first place, so there's a pretty cool party happening at the clubhouse, and everyone is drinking. Coming in as a stranger, I get quite a few looks, but Clover and Felix are quick to tell everyone that I'm with them and that I'm a trusted friend.

"Don't tell them about Constance," Cara whispers to me. "Now is not the time."

"Okay, that's your business. I'm not going to say a thing."

"Sorry you got dragged into my drama before," she says, smiling sadly. "I'm so embarrassed. And to be honest, I'm feeling a little numb right now."

"You don't need to apologize, and you have nothing to be embarrassed about. No one dragged me. I walked right up there and brought myself into it. Something I'm used to doing as an ex-police officer."

"I just don't even know what to think right now," she admits.

"Don't think, just distract," I suggest, giving her the terrible advice I would give myself.

She looks down and smiles. "It's such a small world. I know you told me you knew Felix, but seeing you two together on my home turf? That's wild."

"Yep, I know."

I feel like I've wandered right into the other side of Felix's life. One I had briefly heard about—I knew that his wife had MC ties and that it was a very complicated situation for them, but it seems to have all worked out for him.

I mean, he's still a cop, and right now he's in a biker clubhouse having a drink with Clover's dad, who I find out is a former president of the Wind Dragons MC. Weird. I've known her for years now and I never knew how connected she was to the Wind Dragons.

"Bet you never thought you'd end up here." Cara smirks, crossing her arms over her chest and looking out at all of her friends and family. She points to a man in the corner, one who is currently watching her through a narrowed gaze. "That's my dad."

The man in question brings his eyes to me. "He looks just as happy to see me as your boyfriend was."

She laughs. "You're probably used to that welcome, right?"

I turn to her with a grin. "You might be surprised to know that lots of people find me charming."

She smiles again, and even with her eyes red from crying, she looks beautiful. It's like she radiates warmth, and I don't know how any man could be okay to make her feel the way that Rhett did.

"I don't doubt it. I'm going to get a drink, or ten, as Clover suggested. Do you want one?"

"I'd love one," I reply, watching her disappear back into the kitchen and leaving me standing against a wall alone.

"Who are you?" a woman asks, leaning against the wall next to me. Just by looking at her, I know that she's Cara's mother. She looks just like her. And let's just say that Cara is going to be an attractive woman at any age, because her mother is beautiful.

Cara quickly approaches, two beers in hand, saving me from the inquisition. "Mom, this is Decker. Decker, meet my mom."

"Lovely to meet you, Mrs. Ward," I say, offering her my hand.

"Please call me Bailey."

"Bailey," I correct.

"Where's Rhett?" she asks next, arching her brow at her daughter.

Straight to the point. I like her.

"He's around. I doubt he's coming tonight. He got a bit distracted," Cara says, shrugging. She gives nothing away. It's just like she has flicked a switch and turned all of the pain off. I both admire her for it and worry about her.

"How do you two know each other?" Bailey presses, glancing between us, trying to figure out why the hell I'm standing here right now with her daughter while her boyfriend is nowhere to be seen.

"He's a friend of Felix and Clover's," Cara explains as she hands me a beer.

I thank her and then respond to Bailey, "Apparently that means a friend of Cara's, too."

Bailey's eyes flash with amusement. "I know how it works. Love one, love them all."

I definitely don't love Rhett, but I don't bring that up.

"I thought you weren't coming tonight, but I'm glad that you're here," Bailey says to her daughter.

Cara shrugs. "I wasn't going to, but then I ran into Clover, and you know how it goes."

Bailey nods. "Did you wish Tracker a happy birthday?"

"Yes, I did," Cara replies, turning to me and pointing to a large man with long blond hair. "That's my uncle Tracker over there, and it's his birthday." Uncle Tracker looks like he could be an actor, or a model or something, even though he must be in his fifties.

"You two have a good night," her mom says, kissing Cara on the temple and then heading back to Cara's dad.

"She's nice."

"Yes, she's the best," Cara agrees, clinking her drink with mine. She smiles right at me, brown eyes sparkling—and for a moment, just looking at her, I suddenly feel sober. "I think she likes you. We don't get new people coming around here much, besides the prospects and random women."

"I seem to have that effect on women," I tease.

Cara rolls her eyes, and we join Clover and Felix. I notice myself getting a few looks, but Felix quickly explains that I'm his friend, and that's all there is to it.

We drink, we laugh, and we chat.

I can't even remember the last time that I had so much fun.

The spontaneous nights are always the best ones.

Chapter Six

Cara

I know how inappropriate it is for me to be checking out a man in Rhett's MC clubhouse, but here I am. It's even more inappropriate because I legit just found my boyfriend in a bar with another woman sitting on his lap and kissing him. I don't think I'll ever be able to get that vision out of my head. Part of me wonders if he wanted to get caught. He knew I was going to stop by Rift with Clover tonight.

He says he's too busy to make time for me, but he can find time for other women? I saw red when I saw him, and in that moment I knew that everything Clo said was right.

Rhett and I are the past, and I need to let go so I told him that we were done. I don't think I could ever look at him the same after seeing him with another woman. And if he was there with this one, who's to say he hasn't been cheating on me with other women?

Maybe I've had too much to drink. Maybe I mentally checked out a long time ago with Rhett and now that sparks are flying with Decker, I can't help myself.

I've heard that women do that. They mentally check out long before a relationship is officially over, and by that time, they've accepted that they are ready to move on. Is that what I have been doing?

All I know is that I can't seem to look away from Decker's clear green eyes and his sexy smile.

And considering everything that has happened tonight, it's completely messed up.

Fuck.

I need to get my ass home before I do something that I regret, especially with the whole MC watching me. They know it's unusual for me to be here. It's a school night, and I rarely drink anymore unless I'm on a rare night out with Clover. I hardly come to the wilder events the MC hosts.

But here I am.

Even if tomorrow is the last day of school, which is traditionally more about signing yearbooks than teaching.

I hope Rhett stays all night at Rift and never shows his face here.

Decker and Felix start having a deep chat, so I head to the kitchen to get myself some water. No more alcohol for me—I need to sober up so I can go to work tomorrow without a headache.

"Who's the guy?" Dad asks me, sitting down on one of the kitchen stools. He's dressed in all black, and even though he's in his fifties, he still doesn't look a day over thirty.

"Felix and Clover's friend. Why?" I ask, frowning.

"Rhett isn't going to like you talking with some guy all night, Cara. What's going on?"

My jaw goes tight. "And what if Rhett and I aren't a thing anymore?"

My father's eyes widen. "You've always been a thing."

"I just saw him at Rift with another woman. And Decker and I are just friends," I explain, sighing.

"What?" Dad grits out, cutting me off. "I'll cut off Rhett's dick and shove it down his throat. I don't care if they want him to be president one day—no one disrespects my daughter like that."

"Dad," I groan. "You need to let me handle this, all right? I'm always going to care about Rhett, and him being dickless isn't going to help anyone."

Especially if he is going to become president one day, which is something I wasn't aware of. No wonder he's always busy on club business—he'd have a lot of pressure on him if he's going to be leading these men one day. Not that it changes anything between him and me, but at least I understand more. It just proves that ending things with him was the right thing to do—he doesn't tell me anything.

I sit down next to Dad and lean my cheek on his shoulder. "I'm not happy, Dad. And something has to change. Just because everyone thinks you are meant to be with someone doesn't mean that you have to be. And Rhett's actions tonight prove he's feeling the same. He wants his freedom? Well, he's got it."

Dad is silent for a few seconds, and then lifts my face up to look at his. "You do what makes you happy, you hear me? And I'll always have your back, no matter what. You come first."

Something I always knew but Rhett could never say to me. "I know."

"Do you think Rhett is going to let you go that easily?" he asks, sounding confused. "He'd be a fucking idiot if he does."

"It's my choice. We're not good together. It's probably going to be a relief for him. I know it feels that way for me."

Uncle Arrow comes over and kisses the top of my head. "Bailey just told me not to threaten the new guy. Who the fuck is he?"

I grin. Some things never change, and the Wind Dragons men being protective is one of them.

"He's a friend, and he hasn't done anything wrong," I tell him.

"She keeps defending him, which makes me think otherwise," Dad adds, sharing a look with Arrow. "We should go over and officially introduce ourselves."

"Let's," Arrow says jovially in his deep voice, and the two of them head out to terrorize a man for doing nothing other than speak to me.

I'm about to follow after them and save Decker when Rhett appears. Like my night couldn't get any more stressful.

"I thought you weren't coming here tonight," he says when he sees me.

"And I thought you were a faithful man." I shrug, not offering him any further explanation. "I'm about to leave, though, don't worry."

"I'm not worrying, this is your family too," he says, coming closer and looking down at me. "I'm sorry about before. I shouldn't have been there with her. I fucked up, Cara."

"Yes, you have. We can't be together, Rhett. It's just

not what we both want, and not how I thought my life would be," I admit, as we wrap our arms around each other. "And tonight you proved that you feel the same. We need to stop this cycle from continuing, and I'm not happy. I still love you, I always will. You were my best friend before we were lovers, and you will always be that to me."

Breaking up with a man is easy.

Breaking up with your life-long best friend?

Not so much.

We always thought we'd be together forever. Maybe with so much pressure on us, we were doomed from the start.

But just because I came from this life doesn't mean I'm supposed to end up with a Wind Dragon and all of the drama that comes with that. The other women seem to make it work, though, so maybe it's just me and Rhett. We can't seem to, but we can't seem to fully let each other go, either.

Now is the time we need to.

He swallows and shakes his head. "This can't be the end for us, Cara. You can't give up that easily. No relationship is perfect. We can work on it."

I don't know why he's still in denial about us when it's his actions that have caused this. He might not say it, but with how he's been acting, I know he doesn't want to make this work. He just doesn't want to let go of me either. I'm his safety net, and he doesn't want to lose that. But that's not a reason to stay with someone. I can still be there for him as a friend, just like I was before we got together as a couple.

"We can still be friends," I say, wincing as I realize

how cliché that sounds. "I'm still here for you, Rhett. We just aren't working out. I need someone to put me first, someone who I can trust and rely on. Someone who wants to settle down, get married and have kids."

He ducks his head, because he knows that he's not there yet. He's still planning MC world domination, or whatever they do. He doesn't want to be at home with kids.

"I don't want to fight with you anymore," he murmurs. "We never used to fight."

"I know." Remembering Decker and how he's probably being interrogated by Dad and Arrow, I kiss Rhett on the cheek. "Now you can live your life without worrying about me. Be president and enjoy all that comes with that."

"I don't want to give up on us, Cara. I have hope we'll find a way back to each other."

It sounds like a fairy tale, but I don't know if I believe in fairy tales anymore.

I smile sadly and head back outside, where I see Decker sitting between both men. At least he's unharmed. He doesn't look uncomfortable either, so he must have won them over or he's got a damn good poker face.

"What's going on here?" I ask, pulling up a chair and joining them.

"Just having a friendly chat," Decker replies, green eyes dancing with amusement. He runs his hand through his dark hair and winks at me. "They were telling me how your uncle Arrow here has been to prison for murder."

"Let me guess and he's not afraid to go back?" I add, smirking. Yeah, we've all heard Arrow tell this story to any man he wants to scare away from the women in the MC.

"Exactly," Arrow adds in. "And Cara is a good woman. You won't find any better."

"I thought you were trying to scare me off her?" Decker points out.

"They want you to leave me alone but also to appreciate me," I say, laughing.

Dad shakes his head at me. "My daughter can look after herself. She was raised like that, but the bottom line is if anything happens to her, we will kill you."

"Good to know. And yes, I know she can look after herself. She already almost pulled a gun on me when we first met."

Dad arches his brow at me, while Arrow just laughs, a deep, booming sound. "Well, then. We all know where we stand."

I don't know where the hell I stand.

"Why would you need to pull a gun, Cara?" Dad asks, suspicion racing in his gaze.

"Long story," I admit, wishing we didn't accidentally tell him that part. I give Decker a look and he mouths *Sorry* to me.

Dad seems to accept that for now, and we all continue with our conversation. They're all giving Decker shit, but nothing has happened between us, and I literally just broke up with Rhett, so nothing will. At least not now.

Clover comes over and sits down on my lap. "You all right?"

I nod, and notice her watching Rhett coming outside to join everyone. "I'm fine."

At least, I will be.

I feel sad, like I've failed somehow, and maybe a little disappointed. No one would have expected us to break up. But at the same time, I feel like this is the right thing to do.

Clover kisses my cheek and whispers in my ear, "I don't know who to ask about first, Rhett or Decker."

I laugh under my breath. "Neither is mine."

"Seriously, though, what's going on with you and Decker? You've been by his side all night. I can't believe you two even know each other. Felix has always said he's a good guy, but he's also a bit of a player. So if you wanted to get under someone new, he'd definitely have the experience."

I shake my head in amusement at her advice. "He's a cool guy, we're just chatting. Friends—I'm allowed to have ones with penises."

She throws her hands up. "I'm just saying."

"Aren't you supposed to be Team Rhett? He's your best friend, too."

"Yeah, but I've been Team Rhett for years and after what he pulled tonight, I never should have been. What he did was wrong and I'm done defending him. All I want is for both of you to be happy, and right now, it's obvious you are not happy with each other."

She's not wrong.

Although her added "right now" means that she might think that at some point we could work out. I'm not so sure. For me, I think it's now or never, and with how things are panning out, it's clear we are heading toward the never.

Clover's mom, Faye, comes over and hugs me, her striking auburn hair noticeable anywhere. "There's my gorgeous girl. How are you? And who is this handsome devil?"

"This is Decker." I introduce him to her. "He's a friend of Felix's. He used to be his partner, actually."

"Hot cops everywhere," she murmurs, flashing him a smile. "Nice to meet you. I'm Faye."

"The pleasure is all mine," Decker replies, offering her his hand and keeping eye contact with her, his clear green eyes impossible to look away from.

I can see how he gets so many women. He's handsome and charming, and when he looks at you, it's like he sees right into you. Like he knows what you are thinking and has you all figured out without you having to say anything.

He's a dangerous type, this Decker.

Men like this are both open and closed at the same time. Like he could be friendly, affectionate and warm, but he never truly feels anything on a deeper level.

I know his type.

Men like Decker can't be kept.

They are the ones you get attached to faster than you can imagine, and then suddenly they aren't ready for a relationship or any commitment. They like the fun, the challenge and the chase. And then they are on to the next.

What they don't like is commitment.

Rhett comes over, eyes narrowing when he sees Decker sitting among us. "What the fuck is he doing here?"

Clover scowls at him. "He's *our* friend. You mess with him, you mess with all of us."

And that's how Decker got adopted into the Wind Dragons family.

Chapter Seven

Decker

I don't really know how I find myself in these kinds of situations, yet here I am sitting between two OG bikers. I have to remember to tell Sim about this the next time I talk to her. She'd get a kick out of it.

Then I have another biker, Rhett, who looks like he wants to kill me, and a flurry of beautiful women of various ages milling around, which I'm not going to complain about.

The most beautiful woman of all, though, is sitting opposite me, and defending me to anyone who tries to have a go at me. I wonder if she knows how much I appreciate that. Not because I couldn't handle them myself, but because it's nice to know I have someone on my side. She doesn't even know me, yet she won't let anyone give me a hard time. She's a trustworthy and loyal person, and I can only imagine the kind of partner she would make.

I wonder if Rhett knows that he has made the biggest mistake of his life by letting her go. Some women are one of a kind, and I get those vibes from Cara.

She has beauty, brains and is witty as hell.

What more could you want?

I'm glancing around, taking in the Wind Dragons' no-expense-spared clubhouse, and Cara must notice. "It's had an upgrade," she explains, amusement in her tone. "It never used to be *this* nice."

The Knights of Fury MC clubhouse is top of the line and modern, but this is next level. The Wind Dragons are definitely not short on funds, and everything looks luxurious and brand new, from the black leather couches and the new decked-out bar to their TV, which almost covers the entire wall. Many of the Wind Dragon members are all a bit older than the Knights, and I think it proves they are a legacy.

"It's definitely not what I was expecting," I admit, bracing myself when I see Rhett approaching.

"Stay away from Cara." He seethes when he comes to sit with us, while trying to stare me down.

"Rhett—" Cara starts, but I don't need her to defend me.

"But you two aren't together anymore, right?" I ask, keeping my cool. "Pretty sure you fucked that up without my help. So I don't know why you're angry at me. You should be angry at yourself."

"Ahh fuck," Rake mutters under his breath. He turns to me. "You want to fight it out, you two? We have a gym with a boxing ring."

If we did fight it out, I would win. It doesn't matter how good of a fighter Rhett is, because I've been training in martial arts ever since I was in high school. I even used to compete when I was younger. I'm good. And that's not just my ego talking.

"I wouldn't do that to Cara," is all I say, bringing my eyes to her. "I don't think she needs her night ruined any further."

Rhett's features harden at that dig. His fingers grip at the edge of his leather cut, knuckles going white. He's about to say something to me when the birthday boy comes over and drags him away with his arm around his shoulders. "Come on, let's go have a chat."

Cara sighs and takes a sip from her bottle of water. I don't know when she changed to water, but I should have followed suit. She's clearly more intelligent than me.

Next to me, Rake laughs, big shoulders shaking, and I realize I said that last part out loud. "Damn right she is."

Cara hides her smile behind her palm.

"So what case brought you to town?" Rake asks me, running his hand through his short blond hair. Cara's dad is an intimidating man; I'm not going to lie. These men have been on the other side of the law from me for their entire lives, yet somehow they've allowed me into their world just on Felix's, Clover's and Cara's word of my character alone. They must really trust them.

I try not to look at Cara to give it all away, because it's her business to tell. "Just finding a lost family member for a client of mine. I found her, and so tomorrow I'll be heading back south."

"That's a shame," Clover comments, sharing a look with Cara.

I'm introduced to the rest of the Wind Dragons MC, and there's a shitload of them, their partners and kids. I have a good time even though I can feel Rhett's eyes on me the entire night. I wouldn't be surprised if he tries to start some shit with me when we leave here, or if he manages to catch me alone.

Faye takes a photo of me so she can "discuss me in the family chat." But I take it as a good sign. It means I made an impression.

"I should go home; I have work in the morning," Cara says, glancing at her watch.

"Don't leave me here," I say dramatically, earning myself another grin.

"My car's at Rift."

"So is mine."

"Clover or Felix will have to drive us back there to get them," she says, studying me. "But you won't be driving tonight."

"No, you won't be riding tonight. I'm not a piece of meat, Cara," I say with a straight face.

Her jaw drops. "That's not what I said—"

I burst out laughing, and she shakes her head at me. "What the hell am I going to do with you?"

I mean, I could think of a few things.

"Don't look at me like that," she grumbles, looking away.

"Like what?" I ask, waiting for her to slowly bring her eyes back to me.

She turns her back to me instead, so I walk around her and face her so our eyes are locked once more. "Like you're hungry for something that's not being offered."

"You have beautiful brown eyes, you know that?" I whisper, unable to look away.

She ducks her head, cheeks blushing a little. "You're good, Decker, I'll give you that."

"How do you know? You haven't even tried me yet."

Clover sticks her head into our conversation. "Guys, should we go home? It's getting late, and Tracker and Lana are making out."

I turn to find a woman with dark hair straddling a man, both of them in their fifties, the two of them going at it. While the image may seem a little uncomfortable, it's oddly arousing—which means I probably should go.

"That would be our cue to leave," Cara replies, looking entertained. "Grab Felix and let's get out of here."

We say our goodbyes and pile into Felix's car. I look over at Cara next to me in the backseat and wonder why I can't find any women like her who live closer by.

From the outside it would look like I have no trouble getting women, and that might be true, but I can't seem to find that soul connection with anyone. And when I think there might be something more there, there are usually some kinds of obstacles in the way.

"Are we getting food or going straight to drop you two off?" Felix asks.

"Food, of course," Clover pipes up from the front. "It's the best part of the night, and we have to soak up all that alcohol so we can all carry on tomorrow like responsible adults."

"Pretend, you mean," I add, making them all laugh.

We stop at a twenty-four hour burger joint and share a booth. "I haven't done anything like this in so long," I admit, leaning back against the leather. "It's been all work and no play."

Okay, a little play, usually involving women, but no time for going out with friends or drinking.

"Me too," Felix agrees, wrapping his arm around

his wife. "It's been good, though. I'm glad we made the drive here and ran into you. Who knows what would have happened if we hadn't."

"Rhett would have decked him in front of Rift?" Clover suggests, giggling. "Decked, get it?"

Cara rolls her eyes.

"I know Rhett is a good street fighter, but Decker would have easily won that fight, no doubt there," Felix tells her. "He's a beast; take my word for it. He did Rhett a favor by not getting into it with him."

I grin wolfishly. There is no satisfaction greater than being better than a woman's ex.

"What? No way. I've seen Rhett fight. Hell, *I've* fought Rhett. He's good," Clover replies, shaking her head in disagreement.

"Yeah, he's good, but Decker is fucking great. Remember, I told you he's a martial artist. I know you all train with each other, but Decker is actually professionally trained in muay thai," Felix tells her, looking back at me. "I know he just looks like a pretty boy, but he's not."

Clover's eyebrows rise as she looks me over, impressed. "Oh, shit. That's right. I vaguely remember you telling me something along those lines. Want to fight me, Decker? I've been looking for a challenge."

I laugh out loud. "No, thank you. I don't make it a habit to fight women."

Clover smirks. "I'm not just any woman. I've been fighting ever since I was a kid. And it's the twenty-first century. Gender equality."

"Babe, you can't be mad at him that he doesn't want

to fight my wife," Felix replies in a dry tone. He brings his eyes to me. "Thank you for declining."

"Anytime."

"I appreciate you not taking the bait and putting on a show in the ring," Cara says to me as the food arrives. "Especially now that I know that you easily could have."

"Like I said, I wouldn't do that to you. You had enough of a rough night as it was," I reply, leaning my arm behind her on top of the leather seat. "And I don't really feel the need to fight to prove myself. I'm a man, not a boy. I'm not one that can be easily goaded to do something that I don't want to."

"Good to know," she replies, tucking her silky brown hair back behind her ear.

"Why are you still single, Decker?" Clover asks, taking a sip of her milkshake. "What's the baggage?"

I laugh at her bluntness. Clover always likes to ask me this, looking for a magic reason why I'm single. "Baggage? Where do I start?"

"Clover." Felix sighs at his wife. "You always ask him this."

"Well, everyone has some. And in all the years we've known him, he's never had a serious relationship. He's good looking, and you said he's never had a problem with female attention, and the way he's watching my best friend right now, I think I have the right to ask," she declares, lifting her chin.

"I've told you before, I don't know about any baggage. I don't have any crazy exes still causing me grief, no kids... That I know about," I reply, ignoring her other comment about Cara and thinking about what else could be a deal breaker for some.

"Debt?" Clover presses.

I shake my head. "Nope, you know me better than that. I own my own house and car."

She tilts her face to the side, studying me. "You said that you've never been engaged…"

"And that hasn't changed."

"You've never mentioned any long-term girlfriends."

"Clover," Cara chides.

"One. Nothing too serious."

"Ah ha! That's it then. It's the commitment issues for you," Clover concludes with a smirk. "And you're a ladies' man. The two go hand in hand."

"Or I just haven't been as lucky to meet someone I can connect with enough to want to commit," I fire back. "I'd never be in a relationship just to be in one. I happen to like my own company and I'd rather be alone than with someone who isn't right for me."

And I'm not just going to go around and have babies with a woman who isn't my soul mate. I see it all the time. Men who regret who they chose to be the mother of their children, and all of the hell that comes with that, and vice versa. I want to be sure about the woman I'm going to end up with.

"So you do want kids?" Clover asks.

I nod. "Yeah, of course I do. I love kids. With the right woman, of course."

She smiles and relaxes back in her seat. "Okay."

I laugh. "You satisfied now?"

"Yeah. And you know Felix has always spoken highly of you, and I've always liked you, so there's that. I always felt good knowing he had you at his back. We trust you. What more can you ask for? Welcome to the group." She grins. "Now tell us about why you are here."

I turn to Cara, letting her explain since it's her story. I know I told Felix the quick version of the story earlier, but Clover hasn't gotten to hear it yet.

Cara looks around the table, fidgeting with her hands. "Wade had another child, a daughter. And she hired Decker to find me. That's why he's here," she says.

Clover's mouth opens, and then closes. "So you have another sister."

"Something like that," Cara murmurs.

"There's a lot to unpack there," Clover says.

"I know; I'm still processing it."

"What are you going to do?" Clover asks, brow furrowing. "You know we are here for you no matter what."

"I know. I'm going to worry about it later. Let's just enjoy the rest of the night."

"You sure?" Clover asks, skepticism obvious in her voice.

Cara nods and changes the subject, asking Felix about a case he had been working on.

We finish our meal, chatting and laughing, Cara's warm arm pressed against mine.

This trip definitely took an unexpected turn, but a good one.

What a night.

Chapter Eight

Cara

I wake up feeling warm and safe.

Until I open my eyes. Then I realize I'm pressed up against an almost-naked male form. I'm spooning him from behind and our legs are intertwined, like we're a married couple and completely comfortable with each other. I've never slept like this with Rhett; I usually prefer my own space when I sleep.

I'm still fully dressed, but he has nothing on except his underwear.

I slowly roll off the man and over to the corner of the bed, remembering how we got here. After eating, Felix and Clover dropped us both off at my house, because I told Decker that we could go get our cars together in the morning. Decker had offered to sleep somewhere else, but I told him it's fine because I have a king-size bed that we could just share like any friends would. And normally I sleep very still.

But I'm an idiot, I know. We started off on opposite sides of the bed, and obviously in the night our bodies found each other. Still, nothing happened between us, not even a kiss. Yet somehow the whole night still felt so intimate.

And inappropriate and unfair to Rhett. Yeah, we might have ended it, but that doesn't give me the green light to literally jump into bed, a bed I shared with Rhett, with someone else.

What a hot mess I have become.

My alarm hasn't gone off yet, so it must be before six a.m. I get up and jump in the shower, letting the hot water run over my skin. It's not like me to have drinks or go anywhere on a work night, and now the guilt is hitting me. At least I cut myself off at the right time and don't feel too hungover. I think the water and food last night before bed definitely helped. I know I should have let Decker be dropped off back at his hotel and just let him catch a taxi to get his car, but I do pass by Rift on my way to work, so last night it had just seemed like a good idea.

Maybe I just wasn't ready to say goodbye, I don't know.

I clearly wasn't thinking.

I head back into my bedroom in a towel and, seeing that Decker still seems to be asleep, quickly grab my clothes and take them back into the bathroom to finish getting ready. While I'm in there, I check my phone to find Rhett has sent me a text:

I know you went home with that guy last night, Cara. I got a security alert when you got home. What the hell were you thinking?

Not about him, apparently, and I feel awful. As much as he hurt me last night, I don't want him to think I so callously brought another man to our house. I can't believe I did this.

I don't reply to him.

When I reappear in the bedroom, Decker is sitting up and groaning.

I grin, putting Rhett out of my mind. "Want some coffee?"

"I'd love some," he replies in a deep, husky tone.

I roam into the kitchen, make two coffees and bring one to him in bed.

"I put a towel in the bathroom for you if you want to have a quick shower, and I'll make us breakfast," I say. "I usually have avocado toast and some eggs."

"That sounds perfect, thank you," he replies, fingers reaching out to touch the tips of my wet hair. "You know, the first thing I noticed about you is your hair. It's beautiful."

I clear my throat. "Thank you."

He chuckles as I escape my own bedroom to make some breakfast.

I hear the shower turn on and picture him in there. I know his body is amazing—I had a quick sneaky glance when he undressed to get into bed last night. He's muscular, with abs to die for and a little spluttering of dark hair on his chest.

Stop it, Cara. You just broke up with Rhett and you're in the house you share. Keep the hormones in check.

I almost burn the eggs, chiding myself. "Concentrate, Cara."

I've just placed his plate down on the kitchen counter when he walks out, shirtless of course, just to tease me a little more. He sits down and smiles. "Looks amazing, thank you."

I try to stare at his face—just his face—but my eyes keep dropping to his broad shoulders, perfectly shaped arms and chest.

I can't remember the last time I was this attracted to a man, and I honestly don't even know what to do with it. I can't think straight when he's around.

"So, you going to be coming back any time soon or have we scared you off?" I find myself asking, forcing my eyes to my plate.

He gives me a cocky smile. "You kidding me? I had more fun last night than I've had in a long time. You guys are really lucky to have such fucking amazing people around you. And I tell you what; Clover would take a bullet for you any day. Loyalty like that is rare."

I know. The Wind Dragons MC is built on it, and I've been lucky enough to be a part of that.

I look at him and flash a small smile. "I know, and I would do the same for her. You've known Felix and Clover for years, huh?"

He nods, taking another sip of coffee. "Yeah, Felix is one of my closest friends. I don't know Clover as well, but she always gives me a hard time when I see her."

"I'm sorry if she was nosey last night. She's just a little protective."

"No need to apologize; I respect that. To be honest, I never really shared too much with her when she pried. She was taking advantage of the situation. And you know what? I'm the same with my little sister," he admits, lifting the toast to his lips and taking a crunchy bite. "You know, speaking of my sister, I can't remember the last time anyone made me breakfast aside from her."

"What? Your one-night stands don't feed you in the morning?" I tease, lip twitching.

He puts his piece of toast down and flashes me the most charming smile. "I usually don't stick around long enough for that."

I knew he was going to say something like that. "Yet here you are, sticking around even after we didn't have sex."

He laughs. "You are different, I guess."

Our eyes connect and hold.

I look away first.

"I'm glad I met you. I owe Constance one," he adds.

"I forgot all about that," I admit, wincing. "When do you think you'll be able to get that background check on her?"

He nods. "When I get back home, I'll send you the paperwork and I'll get started. I should have information to you by the end of the week."

"That's great. Thank you. I guess, depending on what you find, I should reach out to her soon."

"You could come and visit her," he suggests, tone playful. "You could stay with me, let me return the favor. Unfortunately I have a guest room, so there'll be no excuse to spoon again, but it's all yours."

Feeling guilty because I also have a guest room, I laugh and shake my head at him. "I thought we weren't going to bring that up, but of course you had to."

"What? I had a great night's sleep. Best in a long time, actually. You even rubbed my abs in your sleep, I found that pretty...soothing."

"Okay, that's enough out of you." I smirk, finish up my breakfast and put my plate in the sink. "I'll go do my hair, and then we can leave."

I put my hair in a high bun and slide my heels on while he washes our plates. Then we both get in my car.

"I like the security you have," he comments as the gates close behind us. "No one is getting in there."

His mentioning of security has me cringing for once again forgetting about Rhett and that he probably thinks the worst of me.

"Yep, you can never be too careful, especially with who my dad is and who I…live with." I can't sugarcoat the awkwardness of the situation. "I think that's why I'm a little worried about Constance reaching out. It's more than likely that she wants something from me, or her dad does. I guess we will all find out soon."

"You should tell your family about it," Decker advises me. "If there's a chance that she might not be genuine, you need your people around you. They'll likely notice something is amiss before you, because they have no emotional investment in it."

"I know. I will tell them—I just wanted to process it first."

"And if you want me to be there when you meet her, to have your back, I'm happy to do that, all right? Anything you need," he says sincerely.

I glance over at him from the corner of my eye. "Okay, and thank you. That does make me feel better."

He pulls out his phone. "What's your phone number? I'll add you and send you a text so you can have mine."

"You're a PI; as if you don't already know."

He laughs. "I'm just being polite. Consent is important."

I tell him my number and he saves it in his phone. We arrive at Rift, and I park just behind his car, the only one still there. "Looks like no one else made any bad decisions last night," I tease.

"Just me apparently, but hey, I met you, and I had a good night. Thanks for everything, Cara. I'll be in touch about the information I find on Constance."

He kisses me on my cheek, flashes me a panty-dropping smile, and then gets out and closes my car door.

I watch him get into his car and drive away. And then I head to work, trying to process my reaction to Seth Decker.

I come up short, because I have no fucking idea.

Maybe I just want to sleep with him.

Maybe I just want to be his friend.

Or maybe, just maybe—I want both.

Either way it doesn't matter what I want. He's leaving and it's probably for the best because I need to work on myself. Being single or alone doesn't scare me at all. In fact I'm looking forward to the change. No more waiting for Rhett to text, or sitting up for him at night, or wondering what he's doing.

Right now is all about me, and figuring out what I want to do with my life.

It's about me being happy.

But first I need to make it through a day of class.

Chapter Nine

Decker

The drive back home is pretty painful, not going to lie. I definitely regret letting loose as much as I did, but I really did have a good time.

I email Constance asking for a meeting, since I'm going to have to tell her I found Cara and that she will get in contact with her when she is ready. Not really the usual protocol—in fact, I probably won't even charge Constance for this case, because I didn't really have her best interests at heart; I let Cara have the upper hand.

And then I let Cara hire me to investigate Constance in turn.

Probably unprofessional, even if all I gave Cara was Constance's full name and contact information.

I send Sim a text checking in, and Nadia calls me just as I get home, asking about how the trip went.

"Yeah, it was good," I say with a wide smile. "As you know, I found our person of interest." And she's now *my* person of interest. "And then she hired me."

"So you went with that, huh?"

"I did."

"I was going to call you to ask if you have decided if you want to become partner, but I'll wait and see how this plays out before that."

I laugh out loud. This has been an ongoing conversation between us, and something I've been thinking about. "Probably smart. You said I can call the shots, so I did. I'm not charging Constance, so that has to count for something, right?"

"Is that how you are justifying it to yourself?"

"Yes. And I have been thinking about your offer."

"And?" she asks patiently. "You can take as much time as you need before you decide. There's no rush."

"I know."

But I have thought about it, and I love where I'm at right now. I love being a team with Nadia and I love that we have each other's backs. Being her partner at the firm is going to ensure me job security, which will allow me to be able to support a family one day. And I do want that. One day.

"I'm going to accept it."

She pauses for a few seconds before speaking. "Are you sure? One fun case and you're all in?"

"Yep. I'm sure."

I can hear the smile in her voice. "Okay, let's talk about it more in person. But I'm glad."

"Me too. Let's make it happen."

We end the call and I jump in the shower, unpack and settle back in.

Clover texts me with some photos from the night before and I can't help laugh at a few of them. There's a terrible one of me dancing, arms in the air, and another of all of us posing. I love that they are all successful, ambitious people but also know how to have a good time and let loose.

Me: Great pics. Are you guys back home too?

Clover: Yeah we just got in! How are you holding up?

Me: Not too bad.

Clover: This is my fave pic of the night.

She resends a picture of me and Cara. We're sitting next to each other in the clubhouse, and she's looking at me and smiling.

I don't know what Clover is playing at. Don't get me wrong, I'd have Cara in my bed if I had the chance, and not just for sleeping—but I also know that Cara just got out of a complicated relationship, so I don't want to put her in that situation.

Timing can be a bitch, and this is just one of those situations.

But fuck, I would love to have her under me.

In front of me.

I'd love to have my mouth…

Thinking about it, I instantly harden, and yeah, it's not ideal that the woman I'm thinking about won't be the one to cure my raging hard-on, but it is what it is.

I've always been torn between being an "if it's meant to be, it will be" and a "nothing will come to you unless you fight for it" person. But with relationships?

If a person is meant for you, they will find their way to you.

And if they aren't? You find someone else.

It's as simple and as complicated as that.

"What is she like?" Constance asks, brown eyes curious. She tucks her hair back behind her ears and waits for me to respond, staring at me over my office desk. She does look a little like Cara, maybe if I squint, but her lips aren't as full, her eyes not as warm. Her brown hair isn't as long, and it doesn't make me want to run my hands through it. I'm probably a little biased. Regardless, I don't get any bad vibes from this girl. I'd be surprised if she was out to hurt Cara.

"She's…lovely," I say.

That seems like a safe word.

Sexy, fucking amazing and *badass* are probably inappropriate.

"And I hope you don't mind how I handled the situation, but she didn't seem too comfortable about it, so I thought it would be better if she came to you."

Constance nods. "Nope, that is perfectly fine. I can't believe how fast you found her and how close she is. I hope that she reaches out soon. I've been wanting to meet her ever since I heard about her."

"You never heard about her before?" I ask curiously. I decided not to charge Cara for looking into Constance either. It just did not feel right to me, especially with my personal attachment.

She shakes her head. "My dad passed away, and I didn't know about Cara until I was going through his things."

I found out about Wade passing when researching Constance for Cara, so at least we know he has nothing to do with her wanting to find Cara. But I'm unsure how Cara will feel about Wade being dead.

"That must have been a surprise for you."

"Yeah, it was. I thought I was an only child up until now."

I can see why she would want to find her half sister, with her dad gone and having no other siblings.

"Sounds like you've had quite the curve ball thrown at you," I say, feeling for her. "I'm sorry about the loss of your dad."

She shrugs. "To be honest, he was kind of a dick."

Looking more promising every moment.

"So you are just wanting a relationship with her then, or…" I press. "What are you hoping to get out of this?"

She nods. "I would just like to meet her and get to know her, yeah. She's all I have left now, as sad as that sounds. I'd understand if she didn't want to, though, so the ball is in her court. No pressure. Even if she doesn't reach out, at least I know that I tried."

She seems sincere about it. There is something a little…sad about Constance. Not in a vulnerable way, but more in a lost puppy way. Like she has no direction. It makes me pretty confident she doesn't have ulterior motives with Cara.

I tell her she doesn't have to pay the invoice, for which she's grateful, and then she leaves my office just as Nadia comes in.

"Welcome back," she says, handing over a coffee and sitting opposite me.

"Thank you," I reply, gripping it tightly. "I needed this."

"I thought you might. Now about the whole partner

thing, are you sure that you've thought this whole thing through? You really want to do this?" she asks, getting straight to the point.

"It wasn't a rash decision. I can't go back to the force, and I'm happy doing this. It will give me something to build and grow. Something that is mine, too."

"I'm happy. There's no one else I could see doing this with me. Logistically, from now on, everything, expenses and profit, will be split fifty-fifty. I'll have my lawyer send over paperwork to make it official."

"Great! Thank you, Nadia, for giving me a place to land."

She smiles, but then is back to business. "We got a few new cases—did you have any preference on which ones you wanted?" she asks, sipping her coffee.

She opens her tablet and forwards me our open cases to look at and discuss. "I'll take the first cheating husband one. It sounds like he hangs out in some shady-ass areas and I don't want you going there," I tell her, even though I know exactly how she's going to react to my comment.

She rolls her eyes. "I've been doing this for a long time, Decker. Don't you start your alpha shit with me because it's not going to work. We're partners—you're not my daddy."

I almost spit out my coffee.

Nadia laughs.

"Hey, you asked," I reply. "Don't worry, there are plenty of cheating spouses out there for the both of us."

She smirks. "You're telling me. I'm so lucky to have Trade. I know without a doubt he would never cheat on me."

"He'd be an absolute idiot if he did." Trade is a good man, an ex-biker, brother to the Knights of Fury MC President and a father of four. He and Nadia raise the kids together, and they are such a beautiful, loving family.

"Yes, he would. I don't know if you read all of the emails, but one requested 'the hot guy' do her case instead of me. Looks like word is getting around," she says. "You going to take that one?"

"Only fair if she requested me," I reply, trying to keep a straight face.

Nadia sighs and leans back in the chair, crossing her arms over her chest and studying me. "No sleeping with our clients. I know you have a thing for the one you are giving a freebie to, but we can't get that kind of reputation. It's not a PI-and-escort service."

"I know." I laugh. Nadia was sure to tell me that the second she considered hiring me. "I won't sleep with any of the clients…that I charge. I know I mess around, but I wouldn't do that to the business."

But half sisters of clients are free game as far as I am concerned. I'm not charging Cara, so she's not an official client. At least that's what I'm telling myself.

"Just reminding you," she says, handing me the case file. "One cheating husband coming right up. I'm going to be working on the elderly lady who is looking for the child she placed for adoption, and the woman whose house got broken into the other night. Cops didn't find anything, but she's sure she knows who did it."

"Interesting. Let me know if you need any help."

"Will do." She pulls her phone out of her black leather bag and checks the time. "All right, I better go.

I have to be at the school. The kids wanted me to go in and do class help."

"How times have changed."

She stands and smirks again. "I don't know, have you met the school moms? They are savages. I'd rather be at the police station hassling the cops for evidence any day."

We both laugh and then she leaves the office.

I get back to work. I set up meetings with all of the new clients I'm taking on, including the woman who requested me and the shady cheating husband. Once the rest of my week is all booked out, I spend the rest of the morning doing some administration work.

My phone rings, and I smile when I see Cara's name pop up. "Hello."

"Hey. I messaged Constance. I told her I could come see her next weekend."

"Straight to business. Not going to ask me how I am today, or what I'm wearing?"

She sighs, like I'm a pain in the ass, but I can hear the smile in her voice. "You're an idiot."

I don't argue with that.

"Do you want me to come with you? And that invitation to stay at my house still stands."

She hesitates for a second. "Thanks, but I can stay with Clover and Felix. It will be nice to spend some time with Sapphire, too."

Right. Of course she'd stay with her best friend. "My offer stands if you change your mind."

"Thank you."

"I checked up on her. She doesn't seem to have a secret agenda, and the background search came up clean.

She doesn't have any criminal history, and she works as a waitress in a bar. She does have a large amount of debt, but doesn't have a lot of money either." I wonder if I should tell Cara about her biological father having passed, or if I leave that up to Constance to share. On one hand, it's their family story, but on the other, I'm sure Cara wouldn't want me to keep any information from her.

"So you are vouching for her?" she asks me after a moment of silence.

"I think so. The debt is a concern, so hopefully she doesn't want any money from you. Be careful with that. I think you should hear what she has to say. We will all be here with you if something goes wrong."

"I know, thank you. How much do I owe you?"

"Nothing," I reply. "You owe me nothing."

"Decker—"

"You could let me take you out for dinner sometime."

"Decker—"

"Only if you want."

She pauses. "Let me think about it."

"Okay. There's one other thing." I hate that I've hid something from her. But knowing that any search of the name Wade Wilson will show that he died, I want to be the one to tell her.

"Yeah?" she asks, dragging out the word.

"Wade. He's dead. I didn't know if I should let Constance tell you, but I thought I would be honest and let you know."

She goes silent for a few seconds. "Thanks for telling me."

"You're welcome. And I'm sorry," I add. I know they weren't close, but it's still her biological father.

"Don't be."

I find myself checking out her social media and the photos on her profile. Yes, I sent her a friend request and now I have access to her inner circle. Her display picture is her sitting on a motorcycle, holding a pink helmet with a big smile.

She truly is a beautiful woman.

I wonder if she and Rhett will reconnect, or if it is truly over. I know she'd still have to see him at all the club events, so it's not as easy as breaking up and cutting that person out of your life.

I don't want to be anybody's rebound, which means it's probably a good thing that Cara won't be staying with me. I mean, she didn't even say yes to dinner, so maybe nothing will happen with us. Maybe we'll just be friends, I don't know. Either way, I know I want her in my life, and I've never felt that way about a woman I've just met before.

I need to stop thinking about her, because it's not going to do me any favors.

When I get a message later from one of my friends with benefits, a woman who is a cop and is known to be extremely wild in the bedroom, I consider accepting her invitation to come over tonight. I have a lot of pent-up frustration and I'd like to relieve it. After thinking about it, though, I decide to decline, which isn't like me at all.

I head out for lunch, and then catch up with a client who wants me to help locate some of her lost jewelry items that were stolen from her residence. Sometimes people turn to us when they feel like the police aren't taking their case seriously, or that the police just don't have enough time and resources to help them to that extent that they want. And being on the other side of that, I get it.

Constance calls to tell me that she will be meeting Cara next weekend, and I act like this is totally new information for me. "I hope it all works out for you both," I say.

"Thank you so much for finding her. And giving her the opportunity to reach out to me first instead was a great idea. I think it gave her time to reflect about it, and be in control of the situation, and she sounded really excited to meet me."

Well, that worked out well, and I'm glad she sees it that way, even though it was just me wanting to make Cara comfortable.

And then I go to the gym for a muay thai training session and work out my frustrations.

Chapter Ten

Cara

I'm not sure if I should have messaged Decker or not, but I mean, we *are* friends, so there is no harm. It doesn't need to be awkward. Nothing happened between us, but I have to admit to myself that I do keep thinking about him. Maybe it's because I haven't been with anyone other than Rhett in so long, or maybe it's because those green eyes make my heart race. I don't know. Not that I'd admit to any of this out loud—I'm even in denial to Clover, who I usually tell my every thought to.

Tonight I'm going to tell my family about Constance. Then next week I'm going to go and meet Constance. I'm nervous, but also very curious. From the conversation we had this morning, I know that she was born three years after me. I'm assuming my mom didn't know about it, because she has never mentioned it, although we never really discuss that side of the family, if I could even call them that.

After work finishes, I head straight home to find Rhett standing at the front of my gate. I wince, knowing that he's not going to be happy that I changed the code on the gate so he can't just come in and out whenever he pleases anymore. I press the button on my keys so the gate slides open and drive inside, while he follows on foot.

He starts as soon as I open my car door. "So I'm not even welcome here anymore?"

"You are—you own half the house. I just prefer it be by appointment, not whenever you feel like it, until we figure out what to do about this place," I say, grabbing my bag from the car, watching to make sure the gates close before I head to my front door. Now that we're broken up, we have to figure out how to split this house. Mental note: never buy a house with someone who isn't your spouse.

"You can have the house," he says.

"We can discuss that later. What are you doing here anyway?"

"I came here to chat with you," he says, following behind me. As he comes closer, I smell his cologne, a familiar scent, one that once felt like home but now reminds me of the past.

I said that we would still be friends and I did mean that, so I let him in and we both sit down on the couch.

"I just feel really shitty with how we left things," he says, resting his elbows on his knees. He pushes his hair out of his eyes and leans back. "And what was with that guy? You with him now? You brought him back to our house, the night we break up?"

I wince. "I'm sorry about that, but it's not what you think. Nothing happened between us. But you have to remember that the night we broke up I witnessed a random woman with her tongue down your throat."

Now it's his turn to wince. I don't want this to be

a tit-for-tat conversation. So I wave the metaphorical white flag. "I'm not with anyone, Rhett," I reply.

"Still can't trust him, Cara. He's a cop."

"Ex-cop, and he was Felix's partner. You trust Felix, don't you?" I fire back. "And this doesn't have anything to do with us, Rhett. We are over, and now we need to heal and move on."

He goes silent, and I wish I knew what he was thinking. "I love you, Cara."

"I know you do. But are you in love with me?" I ask, because I know the answer to that. We started off so strong, so in love, but somewhere along the way we lost that. We lost that obsession with each other—that spark, that chemistry. We no longer want to be around each other all the time. We got used to being apart from each other, and that's why now we can live without each other.

Rhett rubs the back of his neck in frustration.

"You aren't in love with me, Rhett," I answer for him. "Your actions have spoken for you. I deserve more than that. I will always love you, but I'm no longer *in* love with you."

Such a slight wording difference, but it means so much.

It means the difference between friendship and true romantic love.

He looks down at his boots. "I just don't know how you can walk away so easily."

"This has been a long time coming, Rhett. At least a year now we haven't been happy, but we've held on to each other because it's too scary to let go. But that's not a reason to be together. And I know that you have been with other women. There's no point lying anymore."

He lifts his head, blue eyes meeting mine. "I'm so sorry, Cara. I've fucked everything up. I just got so lost in the MC, and then Arrow told me they want me to take over the club one day, and it consumed me. I distanced myself from you, and just did whatever I wanted. I'm sorry. You're the last person that I ever wanted to hurt."

"Yeah, and you never even spoke to me about that. Aren't we supposed to share things with one another?"

He takes a deep breath. "You're right. I just didn't know what you'd say and I didn't know how to process it. It's a lot of pressure."

With that, my annoyance and anger for him are pushed to the back burner. I move over to him and give him a hug. "I bet. You know you can still talk to me about those things. We're friends first. Always. Maybe we were meant to be each other's first loves, and that's it."

And that's okay. There was a lot of pressure on us to last forever, but that's not always realistic.

I kiss his temple. "You know I'm always here for you, whatever you did. We're good. I forgive you."

I don't want to be bitter about us. Yeah, he did me wrong, and now there are going to be consequences of that. He's no longer going to have me by his side as his woman. I'm never going to be his old lady, or the Wind Dragons' president's wife, and I'm okay with that. I never wanted it, and I still don't want it. I never imagined he'd be taking over one day. Not only am I a teacher, but I also don't want my kids having to live their lives the way we did, always looking over our backs and having people wanting to use us against our parents. We didn't have a normal childhood. I don't want my kids to have to go into lockdowns and to be escorted everywhere. I understand with my family ties that my life might always have some sort of threat of danger, but I don't have to have my future children growing up in a clubhouse like I did.

It's the club for Rhett, it always has been, ever since his mom, Tia, married Talon, his stepdad and club member. Rhett had always wanted to be in that world.

And I want him to be happy, even if that's not with me.

"I'm never going to love anyone how I loved you," he says, rubbing his eyes and sighing. "What the fuck am I going to do without you, Cara?"

"Be free," I say with a smile. "And I'm still here for you. I'm not going anywhere."

"Just not for sex."

I tap him on the back. "You have plenty of options for that. And you never know what will happen in the future. If we're meant to be, then we will be." Even though I don't think we're going to end up together, I still believe that.

He squeezes me tighter and then slowly lets me go. He looks at me and smiles sadly. "We'll find our way back together, I know it."

I stay silent so he continues, "You are a good woman. The best."

"I know."

He laughs. "You ever need me, you call me. I'm here. No matter what it is."

"I know," I repeat.

He kisses me once, gently on the lips, and then he leaves.

* * *

My mom, dad and sister Natalie come over an hour later.

Natalie rushes over and gives me a big hug. I haven't seen her all week because she's been busy with work. My sister is a lawyer, and one of the most driven, ambitious people I know. With green eyes just like Dad's and long dark hair, she is as beautiful as she is intelligent.

I'd already called her and updated her on everything that happened with Rhett. She was disappointed—Rhett was like a brother to her—but I told her that they never had to lose that bond just because we are unsure about us.

"What are you cooking tonight?" she asks. "You didn't tell us."

"Well, I didn't have much time, so I ordered us some pizza and wings instead."

"You look tired," Mom says to me, frowning. "Is everything okay?"

"She's probably still hungover," Dad teases, kissing the top of my head. I rest my head on his chest for a moment, and sigh deeply. I'm hungover from life, if that's a thing. I suppose it is, but they call it burnout.

We all sit down around my TV, feet up on the coffee table.

"So I have something to tell you all, which is why I called this family meeting," I start, glancing around the room.

"We know you and Rhett are over, and we just want you to be happy," Mom says, brown eyes worried. "It's his loss, Cara."

"Yes, Rhett and I are over, but that's not what this is about," I reply, shifting in my seat.

"We want to make sure you're okay."

"I am okay, Mom," I say, smiling. "I'm just going through a period of change right now."

"Tia called me," she says, referring to Rhett's mom, whom I love and adore. "She's worried about Rhett."

"Rhett will be fine."

"And you?"

"I will be more than fine."

"Is it about the house?" Natalie asks. "Do you need money to buy him out?"

"Do I need to beef up the security now that you're here by yourself?" my dad interjects.

Crap. Between my parents and sister, they worry about everything for me. I keep forgetting about this damn house.

Mom looks concerned but simply says, "I'm here if you want to talk to me about anything."

"I know. But this isn't about that. I'm aware everyone all met Decker the other night at the party." I turn to Natalie. "Well, you didn't because you were being responsible and not going out on a weeknight."

Natalie smirks. "I heard all about him, though. Aunt Faye even showed me a photo. Tall, dark, handsome, delicious...and green eyes that would make saying no hard."

Dad looks at her and frowns. "You know I'm sitting right here, right? I don't really want to hear about you not saying no, Natty."

She grins.

"So are you and Decker a thing now?" Mom asks, scrunching her nose. "He's hot and seems nice enough, but don't you think it's a little too soon to get into a new relationship?"

"Not after what Rhett did to her," Dad says. "She doesn't owe him anything. He's lucky I don't wring his neck for doing my daughter wrong."

I scrub my hand down my face. If only they'd let me speak, I'd be able to explain this to them faster.

"Decker and I are just friends. I actually didn't know that he knew Felix and Clover at the start. You know he's a former cop—now he's a private investigator. Well, he tracked me down because one of his clients was looking for me. He didn't say anything the other night because I told him not to. I wanted to be the one to tell you first."

"Who is his client?" Dad demands, pulling his feet down from the coffee table in full dad alertness. "I knew something was up when he said you pulled a gun on him. I fucking knew it."

Ah, yes. "Okay, that was a misunderstanding. I caught him following me," I explain.

"Who is his client?" Dad repeats.

"Apparently Wade had a daughter," I say, bringing my eyes to Mom. "And she has been looking for me and wants to meet me. She couldn't find me because I changed my last name, so she hired Decker to find me for her."

My mom looks like she's going to be ill. "I don't know about this, Cara. What does she want with you? We have nothing do to with any of them."

"So you have another sister?" Natalie says, more to herself than me. "I don't know how I feel about this."

"I do. I don't fuckin' like it," Dad announces, shaking his head. "These are not good people, Cara. I wouldn't trust her."

"She might not be anything like Wade," I say, standing up for her. "I mean, she might, and yes, he actually stuck around to raise her, but don't you think I should at least give her a chance and find out? And Wade is dead. He doesn't have any influence over her anymore."

"He's dead?" Mom asks, eyes widening. "I had no idea."

"It doesn't matter if he's dead, he still brought her up," Dad continues, sharing a look with Mom. "What do you think? She wants money?"

"I don't know," Mom replies, still looking a little shocked at my announcement. "I think I would have just preferred this meeting to be about her dating Decker."

I roll my eyes. "I know you guys are wary. I am too. But I am going to meet her and form my own opinion. Her name is Constance, and I already set up a meeting next weekend."

Silence.

"I don't know—" my mom starts.

"Cara, are you sure?" Natalie asks.

"You sure as fuck aren't going alone," Dad booms over the other two. "You have a kind heart, Cara, and I won't have anyone taking advantage of that. It seems I already fucked up by thinking Rhett would do right by you, and he hasn't. No one else is hurting you now—no one is going to get the chance."

"So what, you all think that she has bad blood and is going to screw me over? You know I have that same blood, right?" I fire back, scowling.

"You are nothing like Wade and his family," Mom says gently, reaching out to take my hand.

"And she might not be either," I point out. "I had

Decker do a background check on her. I'm not going into this blind. She's fine. She's not hiding anything. She has a few debts but nothing out of the ordinary."

"We just don't want anyone to hurt you, Cara. I'm sure you can see it from our perspective," Mom says as she puts a hand on Dad's arm to calm him.

"I know, and I love you all for it, but this girl is my half sister, and I want to meet her, at least once, to see what she has to say. Clover will be with me, so I'm going to be safe, all right?"

"Decker did a background check for you? Who hasn't he done a check on? Are you sure we can trust him?" Dad asks, frowning. "I'm going to do a damn check on him, see how he likes it."

I've already decided that I'm doing this, with or without their approval, because it's something I need to do for me. I'm the one who is related to Constance, not them, so they don't know how I'm feeling. I'm not stupid—I'm not going to do anything I'm uncomfortable with, and if she ends up not being a good person or having an ulterior motive, then simple. I won't see her again.

Everyone deserves a chance, and she might be nothing like Wade.

I know I'm not.

I trust Decker's opinion, and he thinks that I should meet her too. I need to do this and they don't have to understand, but if they were in my situation, they would do the same thing.

I know that they would.

I turn to my dad. "I'll be fine. Know that you both raised me to be smart enough to know red flags when I see them, all right? And Clover will be there. You know she won't let anything happen."

I'm an adult now and this is my call.

They don't like it, but they agree to support me.

And I suppose that's what family is all about, right?

Chapter Eleven

Decker

When Felix and Clover show up at my office, I'm eating a doughnut and having my third coffee of the morning.

"Working hard?" Felix asks, smirking. He pulls out a chair for his wife and then for himself.

"You're not a cop anymore, yet you still eat doughnuts and drink coffee. Be more original, Deck," Clover chides.

"I like doughnuts. Why don't you make yourself comfortable?" I tease, closing my laptop and giving them my full attention. "To what do I owe this unscheduled appointment? No work today?"

Felix nods. "It's my day off, so I'm being dragged around by my wife."

Clover glances around the office. "We were in the neighborhood and I wanted to drop in and ask you a few questions about this whole situation with Cara."

"It wasn't even you that wanted to see me?" I ask Felix, feigning sadness. "That hurts, bro."

Felix chuckles and shrugs. "My wife wanted to interrogate you regarding this whole long-lost-sister fiasco."

"Do you think that she has good intentions?" Clover

asks, wrinkling her nose. "Because if not we're going to have a problem. Cara is a good person, and I'm not going to let anyone fuck with her and take advantage of that."

Usually due to client confidentiality, I wouldn't discuss a case with anyone who wasn't directly involved—but I never charged Constance, so technically she was never my client.

And, well, whenever it involves Cara, the lines seem to blur for me.

"I can only go by my own gut feeling, which is that she does genuinely just want to meet and get to know Cara. I did a background check on her, and I asked all of the right questions. I know that Cara's biological father is bad news, but Constance said he passed away and that's how she found out about Cara in the first place, so it's not like he's there to influence her or get her to do his bidding," I tell them.

"Does Cara know that Wade is dead?" Clover asks.

"Yes, I told her."

Clover nods, studying me. "You run background checks on all of your clients?"

Felix looks away, but I don't miss his amusement.

"If I feel the need to," I reply with a straight face.

Clover leans back and grins. "Whatever. You like her."

"I like a lot of people."

Felix outright laughs this time.

"I'm having a dinner on Friday night when Cara gets here—you should come," she suggests.

"You cooking?"

"No," she replies, looking toward Felix. "But he is."

"Okay, I'll be there," I tell them, never one to pass

up a home-cooked meal, even if it's Felix doing the cooking.

This is the excuse I was looking for to see Cara again, even if it's just as friends. I'm okay with that. I just want to get to know her, even if she's not ready to date and nothing comes of it.

"Wonderful," Clover replies, rubbing her hands together.

"We will see you then," Felix says to me, standing and offering Clover his hand. "We have to pick up Sapphire. We left her with Faye for a few nights. Who knows what the two of them are up to?"

Clover waves goodbye with a big smile and then the two of them leave. I reopen my laptop and get back to work. With Nadia only working part-time now, I've taken on a lot of her administration work, but I don't mind it. It's kind of peaceful sitting here alone and getting it all done.

Lunchtime comes around quickly and I head out to grab something to eat with my sister. She gives me a hug when she sees me, and we take a seat outside, enjoying the sunshine. I haven't seen her since I got back into town.

"How was your work trip?" she asks, browsing the menu like she hadn't already looked at it online. I bet she knows exactly what she wants, because she does this every time.

"It was good," I say, smiling at the thought. "I actually ended up partying with some friends."

Confusion flashes in her blue eyes. "I thought it was work. You went there and got drunk? Who are you?"

I laugh. "Well, I did the work, and then I ran into

Felix and his wife and we ended up at a family event of theirs. It was crazy, but I had a good time."

"That doesn't sound too bad at all. Maybe I'll tag along on your next one."

Last thing I'd want is my baby sister coming to an MC clubhouse with me, but I smile and nod anyway. Simone is a beautiful girl and I have no doubt she'd catch the eye of plenty of their men, and yeah, I don't think I'd like that too much. Nope, I think she should end up with someone safe and boring, like a banker or lawyer. Someone who is into the stock market or something.

"How's work been?" I ask. I'm so proud of her for owning her own business. She's always loved animals, and when she told me she was starting a dog-grooming business I'm pretty sure I looked at her like she had grown an extra head. She has a degree in criminology, so it was a little left field. But she made her own path, and I know she's happy with what she does.

"Yeah, really good. I had to hire another person because we're getting so busy," she says with a smile. "Seems I am making quite the name for myself."

"I'm not surprised," I comment. "I'm proud of you, you know that? You knew what you wanted, and you went after it."

"I just wanted to do something a little more fun, and I love being with the animals all day. It's nice that I can make money off that."

"You know what they say, do something you love and you'll never work a day in your life."

"And how about you?" she asks.

"I love what I'm doing now. It's so flexible, and I

can make it what I want. Nadia and I just agreed to become partners at the firm. So it's going to be my business now, too."

"Wow, congratulations," she replies, smiling at me. "That's huge."

I nod. "I know. See, I can commit."

She laughs.

"Do you know what you're ordering?"

She nods without looking at the menu. "Yeah, I looked at the menu online before we got here. I'm getting the prawns."

I shake my head at her predictability.

We order our drinks and meals, and talk shit until all the food is gone. And then we head back to work.

Our work that doesn't feel like work.

Felix and Clover's daughter, Sapphire, or Fire as they call her sometimes, is such a cute kid. I saw her a couple of times when she was a newborn, and she's definitely grown a lot since then. When I arrived for dinner, it was just Felix and Fire here. Clover and Cara had ducked out to pick up some dessert.

"Bet you have a hard time saying no to her." I smirk as Fire turns to me and smiles.

"You have no idea," Felix grumbles, laughing when she runs up to him and hugs his leg. "But I love being a dad. Something about creating this little life, one that is half me and half Clover... I mean, it doesn't get any better than that, does it?"

"Well, when you put it like that," I mutter, and take a sip of my beer. "Is it just us coming tonight?"

Felix stills. "The girls didn't tell you? They invited

Constance to come tonight, so that we'd all be here to suss her out."

My eyes widen. "Nope, that part was conveniently left out."

Felix laughs and places his hand on my shoulder. "You thought it was going to be a nice, normal, chill night where you and Cara could drink, and flirt, and stare into each other's eyes? Sorry."

Not that I'd admit it, but yes, I kind of did think that.

"You don't think it's weird that I'm here for this? I'm her PI, and now bam—'oh by the way, I kind of know all of these people.'"

Felix laughs again and shrugs. "Decker, I don't know what the fuck is going on tonight, but it's definitely not going to be boring. I really hope she's a nice girl, because Clover is extremely protective of Cara. And Clover is…let's just say even I make sure to not get on her bad side."

"She's worse than Cara?" I ask, blinking slowly as I remember her almost pulling out that gun on me like a total badass.

"They are as bad as each other, and when put together, they are double the trouble. They were both raised the same way. They were taught how to fight, how to use weapons…everything. They aren't MC members, but let's be real, they might as well be. That was their life."

"Yeah, but Cara is a teacher, and Clover was a cop turned FBI agent," I point out. "They are definitely making their own mark in the world."

Felix nods. "One hundred percent. But you can take the girl out of the club…"

But you can't take the club out of the girl.

"It's always going to be a part of them," I say, understanding what he means.

"Yep."

Fire comes and sits next to me, and rests her little head on my leg, her long, dark lashes crescents on her cheeks as she apparently starts to take a nap. I don't know much about toddlers, but she's pretty damn cute.

"She does that," Felix whispers, smiling down at his young daughter. "Just falls asleep anywhere. She must really like you, though. She normally only does that with Clover's family or mine."

I don't have much experience with children, so it's nice that he thinks that.

Cara and Clover come back with cheesecake and brownies, Clover gasping when she sees her daughter resting on me. "Oh my God, that is the cutest thing."

I look next to her to Cara, who is also smiling at me with gentle eyes. "That's pretty cute."

"And he's good with kids," Clover mutters, putting the dessert on the dining table and coming over to pick up Fire. "I'll put her in her bed."

Cara sits down next to me on the couch. "Hello again."

"Hi. I'm only just finding out that this isn't just a casual catch-up dinner," I say, raising my brows.

She covers her laugh with her palm, trying to contain it. "I'm sorry. Clover insisted we do it here so I'm not alone when I meet her. I don't know what she thinks could happen, but here we are."

"How are you feeling about it?" I ask, taking in her

face, her glossy lips and kohl-lined brown eyes. She looks beautiful tonight in her tight jeans and white top.

"I'm a little nervous," she admits, pursing her lips. "I don't know. She's my blood, but also a stranger. We might not even like each other. The whole thing is really weird, but I know that I'm doing the right thing by meeting her."

"I'm here for you," I tell her quietly.

She nods. "Thank you."

A knock at the door has all our heads turning. "Do you want me to get it?" I ask, like I live here or something.

"No, it's okay, I will. It will give me a minute with her before Clover starts in on her," she grumbles, getting up and heading to the door.

Felix and I watch and wait.

Who knows how this night is going to turn out?

Chapter Twelve

Cara

I open the door to a pretty, brunette woman.

I've always been told that I'm a spitting image of my mother, but I must look like my biological dad a little too, because Constance has some facial similarities to me. We both have brown eyes and hair, although hers is shorter than mine, and I can see that our face shapes are a bit similar and we have the same full lips. It's obvious that we are related.

She has a bottle of wine in her hands, and she looks nervous as she shifts on her feet. "Cara?"

I nod and smile. "It's nice to meet you, Constance."

"Please, call me Con." She smiles back and then asks shyly, "Can I hug you?"

"Of course." I grin and open my arms to her.

She holds me tightly and takes a deep breath. "Thank you for agreeing to meet with me."

"Thank you for agreeing to do it here at my friend's house," I say, stepping away and opening the door. It must be hard for her to walk in and not only meet me, but my friends all in one night. She must be really out of her comfort zone, and I do appreciate the fact that she came anyway. "Come on in."

"No problem, I actually live not too far from here," she comments, glancing around Clover and Felix's big-ass house as she enters. Clover lives on a large property, so large that she has to drive when she goes to visit her neighbor's house. "Although my house looks nothing like this one."

I lead her into the living room and introduce her to everyone. "Con, this is Clover, my best friend, and her husband, Felix, and you already know Decker, who ended up being Felix's friend. Small world, isn't it?"

Con grins awkwardly. "It definitely is. Nice to see you again, Decker."

"You too," he replies with a smile.

She hands Clover the bottle of wine. "I didn't know what to bring, but I didn't want to come empty-handed."

"Thank you, that is very thoughtful of you," Clover says as she accepts the bottle. The rest of us all sit down. "I'll go get us something to drink. We have wine, beer, juice, soda. Anything you like," Clover offers Con, being very sweet. A little too sweet.

"A soda sounds great, thank you."

"Wonderful." She disappears into the kitchen and Felix follows her to help.

Decker looks like he doesn't know if he's supposed to disappear too, so I decide to break the ice. "So tell me about you, Con? How did you find out about me? Did you know your whole life? Are you close to that side of the family? I want to know everything." I smile, trying to put her at ease.

Con swallows and looks away. "I only just found

out about you a few months ago. Dad passed away—he died of a heart attack. I was cleaning out his office when I found some documents about you, a copy of your birth certificate and some photographs. So that's how I found out."

I knew Wade was dead. So it's not him sending Con here on some mission to get something out of us. She must have really just wanted to meet me.

"I'm sorry," I say.

She smiles sadly. "He wasn't the best dad, but after my mom died, he was kind of all I had. And now there's just me. I'm not too close with the rest of the family. I have a few cousins I keep in touch with, that's it."

So she's all alone. No parents.

Just a half sister she's only just meeting.

"I'm glad you reached out," I reply, reaching out and taking her hand. "I've never really considered Wade my father, more like just a sperm donor, but it's nice to see that something good could come out of my connection with him."

Con beams. "Thank you for saying that. I wasn't sure if you would want to meet me, because of Wade."

Clover and Felix come back with drinks and a cheese platter. I have no doubt Clover was listening in from the kitchen. I know my best friend more than I know myself.

"So Con, what do you do for work?" she asks, placing a can of chilled soda in front of her.

"Thank you. Um, I'm a waitress at a bar," Con says, opening her drink. "I was in college, but when Dad died I dropped out and started to work full time to pay for his house or the bank was going to take it."

"What were you studying?" I ask.

"Business."

"Cara has a degree in marketing and advertising on top of teaching," Clover adds, smiling at me.

"Wow, that's impressive. But teaching was your calling?" Con asks, picking up a grape from the platter and popping it into her mouth.

"Yeah, I love being a teacher. My mom was one, and I saw how much joy it brought her. It's a hard job, but the rewards are high."

"My mom was a stripper," Con blurts out, and then clears her throat.

It's painfully obvious that she had a completely different childhood than me. Yeah, I grew up with a bunch of bikers, but I was afforded every opportunity. Money was never an issue and education was always important. We were a very close family and there was so much love there. Rake was the best dad I could have asked for because he was always there for me and treated me like his own. I always knew I was lucky, but hearing what my life could've been had things happened differently puts it a bit more in perspective.

"There's nothing wrong with being a stripper," Decker comments, also clearing his throat. Felix starts to laugh under his breath. I don't miss Decker shooting him a look that clearly says *shut up*.

"What's so funny?"

"Nothing," Decker replies, lips tightening.

"You just said there's nothing wrong with it, why can't I tell them?" Felix asks, shoulders now shaking as he tries to contain himself.

"Spill," Clover demands of her husband.

Decker turns to me. "I used to do a little stripping while I was in the police academy."

My eyes widen and I hear Clover mutter, "You never told me that, Felix."

I suddenly imagine him standing up on a stage, horny women eying his naked body, and my stomach drops.

Yeah, I don't like that thought at all. If I didn't know better, I'd think I was a little jealous at the thought of so many other women seeing him like that.

"Cara?" Decker says, and I wonder how long I zoned out for, or if my expression gave my thoughts away.

"Yeah, sorry, still processing the stripper thing."

"It was a short-lived career," Decker chokes out. It's a little cute, the first time I'm seeing him embarrassed. Felix notices and decides to put him out of his misery.

"So Cara is your only sibling?" Felix asks, placing his beer down on the table as he changes the subject. He has a calming quality, something one would need if they married Clover, and I'm grateful for it right now.

"That I know of," Con replies, laughing uncomfortably. "It seems like my dad wasn't the most upfront with information. If he had told me I had a sister, maybe we could have seen each other over the years. Do you have any other siblings?"

I nod. "I do, I have a baby sister, Natalie. She's your age, actually."

"That must have been really nice," Con replies, tucking her hair back behind her ear. "I always wanted to have a sibling. I remember telling Dad that, and you would have thought that might have been an opening to tell me that I already did."

She wouldn't know about how Wade tried to extort

money from my family by using me, and I don't want to tell her about that. Wade is dead, and there's no point speaking ill of the dead, even though I don't have any love for the man.

"I guess to him I wasn't really his kid," I say with a shrug. "It is what it is."

Wade did me a solid by leaving me alone. He allowed me to have a wonderful father in my life and to grow up being raised right. I don't have any bitter feelings about him raising Con and not me.

After another hour of chatting, we head to the dinner table, where Clover and Felix bring out all of the food.

"You made this?" Decker asks Felix, sounding surprised. "When we were partners, you acted like you couldn't make toast without burning it."

Felix laughs, eying his roast chicken with pride. "When you have a woman who loves to eat, you learn how to cook."

"I'm impressed," Decker tells him. The two of them and their little bromance is a little bit cute.

"What about you, Decker? Can you cook?" I find myself asking.

"I can feed myself," he admits, laughing. "But to be fair, I haven't got a woman who loves to eat, so I haven't been forced into that position yet. It's been the bachelor life for me. My sister cooks for me, though."

"He's been the one putting women into positions," Felix mutters, laughing at his own joke.

Con leans closer to me. "He's hot, isn't he?"

"Who?" I ask back, even though I can see her eyes are on Decker.

"Decker. When I went to meet him, I almost died. He's an extremely sexy man."

My hackles instantly rise.

Wow.

I don't know why, but her words set me on edge. I don't like hearing her say that about Decker, which makes no sense, because he is a single man and she's just making an observation.

A correct one. Decker *is* sexy. Guess in addition to blood, we share the same taste in men as well.

"Yes, I suppose he is," I reply, clearing my throat.

"Do you have a significant other, Con?" Clover asks, as if reading my mind somehow.

"Nope, I'm single. I…" She hesitates and shrugs. "I have bad luck when it comes to men. I always choose the wrong ones, so I've decided to stay single for some time now. It's been working out for me so far. I mean, besides the whole getting laid thing."

"Yeah, that's unfortunate," Clover mutters under her breath.

"The right person will come along when the time is right," I add, flashing her a gentle smile.

"I think so too," she agrees. "How about you?"

Suddenly all eyes are on me and I wish this question was never brought up.

"It's complicated," I reply. I glance up and lock eyes with Decker, who is already watching me.

"Isn't it always," Con replies, picking up on my vague answer. We finish up our meal and then I head into the kitchen to help Clover bring out the desserts.

"What do you think?" I ask. "I mean, Wade is dead and she has no other close family."

"I don't know," Clover replies, wrinkling her nose and leaning her hip against the kitchen counter. "I feel like she's not evil, but she might suck the life out of you. I think she's one of those people who just will take advantage of whatever she can to get up in the world. She hasn't asked you for anything yet, but wait and see. I think something will be coming. I'm just going on my gut feeling here."

"She hasn't had the opportunities we did, Clo, that's not fair," I whisper back with a frown. "She's my sister."

"I know. I'm just saying be careful, Cara. Don't let anyone take advantage just because they share half of your DNA."

"I won't," I promise.

"I just have a bad feeling like you might regret letting her into our world," she says quietly, scanning my eyes. "I mean, her name is literally Con. But please, prove me wrong."

She leaves the kitchen and I'm left with a sick feeling in my stomach.

Is she right? Will I regret meeting Con and bringing her around the people I love?

They say no good deed goes unpunished.

Only time will tell.

Chapter Thirteen

Decker

The evening isn't as awkward as I expected it to be, especially after we've all had a few drinks. Cara and Con seem to get along like a house on fire, but I can tell that Clover isn't as convinced. I don't think it's a bad thing that she is protective of Cara and isn't accepting Con after just one meeting. We all need a friend like Clover.

"So what's going on with you and Cara?" Felix asks me when we have a moment alone in the kitchen.

I glance around before I answer. "Nothing. She literally only just became single. I don't think now is the time."

"Since when have you ever cared about being a rebound?" he replies, eyes widening. "You like her."

"I like lots of women."

"I mean you really *like* her. You normally don't think twice about anything. I know you, Decker, and I've seen you work. Damn, even a few times I was impressed with how fast you managed to get a woman into bed."

I cringe, realizing how bad that sounds. "She's your wife's best friend. Did you ever think that I don't want to make it messy for you?"

Felix blinks. "Yeah, that doesn't sound like you at all."

Clover steps into the kitchen and purses her lips. "I can't find anything to complain about Con except a gut feeling. And I don't think that is going to cut it."

"Maybe she is just a genuine person," Felix says, wrapping her in his arms. "We'll be here for Cara no matter what happens. But you can't protect her from everything."

"I know," she replies, her voice muted by Felix's shirt. She lifts her face. "And we'll be here to pick up the pieces. I'm also not opposed to punching Con in the face."

"We know," Felix says in a dry tone. "Hopefully it won't come to that."

Clover looks over at me. "So what's going on with you and Cara?"

I scrub my hand down my face. "Nothing."

"Ten bucks they sleep with each other in the next few weeks," Clover says to Felix.

"You're on. I say this week."

I open my mouth, and close it. While I wouldn't be opposed to Felix winning that bet, I don't know. For once I'm a little out of my element with a woman. I don't know how to approach what may, or may not, be going on with Cara and me.

"We all just going to pretend that Rhett didn't exist? Isn't he your best friend, too?" I ask Clover.

"Yeah, but he didn't do right by her. He let her learn to live without him. I love him, I really do, but he got himself into this situation. He lost the best woman he's ever going to get because he was too busy in the club life. So Rhett is not an issue here. Cara has been getting over him long before she would have ever even admitted that to herself."

Cara's musical laugh makes all of our heads turn.

"Come on, we better go in there. We are being rude hiding in here," I tell them both.

I sit back down next to Cara, and she turns to me, big, brown eyes filled with happiness. "Do you have to work tomorrow?"

I shake my head. "Nope I'm taking the weekend off, why?"

She lifts up a bottle of tequila off the coffee table. It's the one with the scorpion in the bottom of the bottle. "Shots?"

Damn, these teachers are wild.

I glance up at Clover, who perks up a little. She turns to Felix. "One of us has to stay sober and be a parent. We should flip a coin."

Felix smirks, amusement dancing in his eyes. "You can have a drink, babe. I'll take one for the team."

She rubs her hands together menacingly. "Wonderful."

"I mean, I guess I could have one," Con replies, smiling widely. "But I do have to drive home."

"One it is," Cara replies.

Clover brings out some shot glasses and pours the first round.

"To family," Cara toasts, and we all do the first shot, licking the salt and sucking on the lemon to finish.

"Just one, right?" I comment.

"Why am I always drunk whenever you are around?" I ask Cara, closing my eyes and leaning my head back against the leather couch. "You are a bad influence on me, you know that?"

She laughs. "I'm sorry, I actually haven't drunk this much in a long time. Probably because my life is in shambles right now and I have no idea what I'm doing, so having a drink does sound appealing."

"Your life isn't in shambles, you're just going through change. You'll adapt, and you'll be happy again. You're a butterfly, but you've gone back into your cocoon for a little while. Nothing wrong with that."

She turns her head to me and smiles just as I reopen my eyes. "Yeah, you're right. I will adapt. A breakup and a long-lost sister in the same month has kind of thrown me for a curveball, though, not going to lie. And then there's you."

"Me?"

"Yeah, you," she sighs. "You're sexy as hell, and I kind of want to rip your clothes off every time that I see you, but I know it's not a good idea and—"

I groan, cutting her off. "You saying that to me right now isn't a good idea."

"Why not?" she asks.

I lick my suddenly dry lips. "Because we've had too much to drink."

Although I'm suddenly feeling sober right now.

And I'm hard as a fucking rock.

I knew we had a connection, don't get me wrong, but I never thought that she would openly admit it. I'm surprised. There's an undeniable sexual tension between us, and I thought we were just ignoring it and pretending it wasn't there.

But now she's brought attention to it and I'd love nothing more than to have a taste of her.

"I haven't drunk too much that I don't know what I'm doing," she comments boldly, touching my arm with her fingers. "In fact, sober me was thinking the exact same thing the second I laid eyes on you."

"Cara," I whisper.

She brushes her lips against my cheek, such a small touch, but one that sends shivers all over my body.

I glance over at Clover and Con, who are playing a game of cards, while Felix has gone to put Sapphire back to sleep after she started to stir. No one is really paying attention to us, and I wonder if they would notice if Cara and I left and headed to my house.

I clear my throat. "I should probably get going."

Alone.

I should leave here now because if I don't, I know exactly what is going to happen.

Clover lifts her eyes away from her deck of cards. "You can't drive."

"I can drop you all home," Con offers, putting her hand down. "I only had two drinks all night and have had only water since then."

Cara's mouth drops. "What about the shots?"

"I didn't drink them. I just clinked the shot glass against yours and then put it down," she admits, shrugging. "I have to work tomorrow."

Clover finds this hilarious, laughing loudly.

I get up and say bye to Clover, and head outside to get into Con's car, an older model white Pontiac.

"Okay, and where are you going?" Clover asks Cara as she follows me outside.

"I'm going to stay at Decker's," she says casually, like she does it all the time.

Clover smiles slowly. "Is that right?"

Cara nods. "Yeah, don't wait up. I'll be home in the morning."

Clover turns to me, and I nod. "I'll bring her back. I have to come and get my car anyway."

"Be safe!" she calls out and then heads back inside.

I sit in the back so Cara can sit up front with her sister. "Where do you live?" she asks.

I rattle off my address and Con puts it into her GPS, and off we go.

Con stays quiet, and I know she wants to say something, but she doesn't. She's probably wondering why Cara is casually going home with the man she hired to find her, or maybe she's wondering why the whole night we acted like we were just friends yet now she's coming for a sleepover.

I'm sort of wondering the same things.

We get to my house, and I thank Con for the lift. I get out and open the door for Cara. I know this isn't the best idea, but I'm kind of sick of fighting my attraction to her.

"Thanks," she says, getting out of the car.

I close the door, and we both wave and then walk up my driveway together.

"You did offer me your house to stay at," she reminds me.

I smirk as I unlock the door. "I did."

Although this wasn't what I had in mind, exactly.

As soon as the door is shut behind us, she pushes me back against it and kisses me.

No, this is much, much better.

Chapter Fourteen

Cara

I'm sick of overthinking everything. I want Decker, and I'm single and so is he, end of story. We aren't hurting anyone by giving into this tension that has been driving me insane since I met the man and pulled a gun on him. I know I'm taking the lead here and making the first move, but I don't care.

I want him and I know he wants me too, so let's just stop playing games and both take what we need from each other, even if it's just for one night.

Only I don't know if one night is all I'm looking for from him.

I'm on my tiptoes. He lifts me up and turns around so I'm pressed against the door, and kisses me back. I wrap my legs around his hips, while my hands frame his face. He smells so good, like spicy cologne and leather, and he tastes even better.

He pulls back and stares into my eyes for a second like he's silently asking if we're really doing this right now. And I love that we have this shorthand. That with just one look I know what he's thinking and he knows what I am thinking. It's magical, or at least my drunk brain thinks that.

I nod.

That's all it takes, and he carries me through his house into what I'm assuming is his bedroom. He throws me down on the bed and lands on top of me, his lips back on mine and our bodies pressed against each other. I can feel how hard he is, and how big he is, and how much he wants me, and it's so fucking sexy.

I pull at his T-shirt until he takes the hint and takes it off, revealing his delicious, smooth and muscular chest and abs. The only light in the room is coming from the open window, the moon letting me see just enough, and allowing me to feel the rest of him. He kisses along my jawline, and then down my neck, biting gently and sending shivers down my spine. I'm so attuned to his every move, his every breath, and I'm so turned on that he could just slide into me without any foreplay right now.

When he reaches my breasts, he pulls my top off and I sit up to assist. My white bra comes off next, and he makes a deep growl in his throat as he studies me. I unbutton my jeans and slide them down, and he laughs under his breath at my enthusiasm. Once I'm completely bare to him, he continues his torture, kissing my breasts, licking my nipples and then roaming lower.

When he spreads my thighs and starts licking my center, I can't help the moans that start pouring from my lips. Rhett is the only man I've ever been with, so this is so new for me, so exciting, and I'm so fucking ready for it.

"Decker," I whisper as I'm about to come, his tongue on my clit. My hips arch off the bed, but his big hands hold me in place while he draws out every last wave of pleasure.

When my body relaxes against the mattress, he gets off the bed and removes his jeans and boxers, allowing me to stare at him in his full glory. He opens the drawer and pulls out a condom, opens it with his teeth, and slides it on before returning to the bed.

Feeling bold, I sit up, push him back on the bed and straddle him. He made me come, and now it's my turn. Holding his cock in my hand, I guide him into me and slowly slide down, feeling every ounce of pleasure as he fills me.

"Fuck," he grits out between clenched teeth at the same time I moan in ecstasy. Once he's fully inside me, I lean forward and start moving my hips, lifting up and down, bracing my hands on his chest. He lifts his hips in sync with me, and it feels so fucking good I move faster and harder. We're so perfectly in rhythm it feels like we've been doing this for years.

He suddenly flips me over, taking back control, and kisses my neck as he thrusts in and out. The sex we have is uninhibited and unrestrained, and it's like he knows what I want and need from him without me actually saying the words. He reads my body and goes with it, and I his.

After I climax again, he turns me around to enter me from behind and makes the sexiest sounds ever, little deep groans until he finishes himself.

When he slides out of me, I slump onto the bed and catch my breath while he heads to the bathroom.

"Holy fuck," he whispers when he returns, lying down next to me.

I close my eyes and smile. "See? That was a good idea, don't you think?"

He laughs and pulls me into his arms, cuddling me. We both fall asleep.

But not much time passes before we're both reaching for each other again.

"This room looks like a bomb hit it," I comment the next morning after we wake up, sitting on the edge of his bed. The lamp has fallen on the floor from his side table. There are pillows and clothes thrown everywhere, along with condom wrappers and bottles of water we got from the fridge in the middle of the night to rehydrate us.

"I know," he replies, in both an amused and smug tone. He sits up and scans the carnage. "That's when you know that you had a good time."

A good time is an understatement.

Decker worshipped my body and made me feel so comfortable that I wasn't shy in the least. We had sex four times during the night, and to be honest, I could probably go for another round right now.

He stands up in all of his naked glory, and I take the time to study him in the morning light. He's perfect. He's all muscle, smooth skin, and a nice round, tight ass that I want to take a bite out of. He has no tattoos, which is unusual nowadays, but I find the bare, tan skin really sexy on him.

"I'm going to make us some breakfast," he says when he reaches the door. "Any requests?"

"Coffee?"

He grins. "Of course. Bacon and eggs sound good?"

"Perfect."

He disappears and I head into the bathroom to have a quick shower and freshen up. I know that I'm going to have to answer a lot of questions from Clover about my rash decision to basically invite myself over here last night, but I don't regret it one bit.

I exit the bathroom in nothing but a white towel, only to see that Decker left out one of his T-shirts and boxer shorts for me to wear. He comes off as such a bachelor, a playboy, but I'm comforted by how thoughtful he can be.

I put on his clothes and find him in the kitchen, frying bacon in nothing but some boxer shorts. "You like to live dangerously, don't you?"

He turns around and smiles, and it makes me want to drag him back into that room. Or hell, that kitchen counter looks pretty appealing.

He picks up a mug and hands it to me. I put my phone down on the counter to take it from him. "Coffee for you, white with two sugars. And yeah, a little burning oil isn't going to intimidate me."

I grin and take a seat, blowing on the hot liquid. "I remember you saying last night that you aren't so good in the kitchen."

But the view looks pretty damn good from here.

"I mean, this is just frying. Anyone can do that," he replies, amusement dancing in those green eyes of his.

Green is such a dull word for the color they are. The color of the ocean around a tropical island destination. Clear and inviting. I have no doubt that many women have gotten lost in those eyes, and had their heart broken by them too.

Decker serves up our breakfast and we sit side by side to eat it.

"I'm surprised Clover hasn't called yet," I say, taking a bite of the bacon.

Decker grins. "How do you feel after finally meeting Con?"

I cringe, remembering how I got her to drop me off here last night. Probably not the best first impression to make for my little sister. "I thought she was cool. I know she has grown up differently from the way we all did, but none of that matters to me. As long as she's a good person, that's all that I care about. And I think that she is. What did you think?"

"I thought she was nice," he agrees, nodding. "I know Clover will have her walls up about her for a while, but I don't think that is a bad thing either. It takes a while to really get to know someone."

"You're right. I do want to see her more and get to know her, though. She doesn't have any other family left."

"You're a good person, Cara."

My phone rings from where it sits on the counter between our plates, and our eyes both go to it. I was expecting Clover's name to pop up, but no, it's Rhett calling me.

I ignore the call.

"Sorry about that," I mutter, wincing at the timing.

Decker goes quiet, and I know he's thinking about the situation we've gotten into.

I'm a mess, and my life is a mess, and now is not the time to start something new with anyone. I've only just broken up with my one and only long-term boyfriend, the person I thought was my forever. And I should be single and spend some time finding me before I get into anything else. At least that's what logic tells me.

Decker is a little distant after that, and I completely understand why. There's a reason we were both hesitant to jump into bed with each other—the timing is all off.

But we did anyway, and I know I'm the one who initiated that.

We're silent as he calls a cab to take us to Clover's to drop me off and to pick up his car, with me still in his T-shirt. Talk about a walk of shame.

Clover comes out to meet us, smiling when she sees me. "There you are. Have a good night, you two?"

I clear my throat. "Yes, I did, actually."

She smirks and turns to Decker. "You coming in, or you have to head off?"

Decker shifts on his feet. "I think I'm going to head home. Thanks for the invite, though."

He turns to me and reaches his fingers out to touch mine. "Have a safe trip home."

I smile, but don't say anything. Clover and I watch him until his car disappears from sight.

"Safe trip home? You didn't tell him you were moving here?" Clover asks, still looking out at the road.

Shit.

"It never came up." And I only just decided this yesterday.

I need to sort out my head and my feelings and figure out what the hell I'm doing.

Clover sighs and threads her hand through mine, leading me inside. "Tell me all about your night. No detail is too small." She pauses and laughs to herself.

"There are no small details to be told."

"I knew he was packing," she announces, just as Felix opens the door, eyes narrowing on her.

"What did you just say?"

"Nothing," she lies, flashing him a big smile. "Just escorting Cara inside and asking her why she didn't tell Decker that she was moving here."

I didn't really know how to tell him that Rhett also half owns the house I live in, and that now I'm going to have to sell it or buy him out, which I can't afford without asking my parents. Something I do not want to do. And even if I did have the money, I don't know that I'd want to stay there. It has too many memories.

Nope, I'm going to pretend all of those things aren't happening, and I'm going to hide at my best friend's house until I know what my next move is going to be.

I quit my job at the high school because it's the end of the school year, and that gives me plenty of time to find another job.

Decker knows my life is a mess, but I don't think he knows that it's this bad.

If he's smart, he will run while he can.

Chapter Fifteen

Decker

I spend the rest of the day having flashbacks of the night before. Cara surprised me. She was wild. She was confident, bold and knew exactly what she wanted. She was untamed. And I loved every second of it. It's like our bodies were meant to be pressed up against each other.

Reality came to a halt when I saw Rhett calling her. It was a reminder of the situation we're in. What a fucking dilemma. I've never been in this position before. I usually can go about my business without worrying about getting attached to someone, but this time it's different, and I need to be cautious here so I don't end up disappointed. I do not want to be her rebound, yet somehow that's exactly what I have become. Could we just go back to being friends after this? After I've tasted her? If I want something more than sex from her, I think we're going to have to try.

And who am I?

I've never considered a relationship with any of the women I've slept with over the last few years, no matter how beautiful, or intelligent, or witty they had been.

But with Cara?

Something is different about her. I've been fighting it. I should have told her no last night, but I couldn't, and I can't even find it in me to regret it.

I get hard just thinking about it.

Sleeping with one woman for the rest of my life never sounded appealing to me until this moment. And that is why I need to distance myself, because this is a situation that I can't win.

She needs time to heal. Or, hell, for all I know she and Rhett will eventually get back together. I don't know. With her not living in town, it will be easy for me to go about my daily life, not seeing her, and only having minimal contact.

It's been a long time since I've thought about a woman so much, and distraction is going to be key for me to control that.

I flash to her bent over in front of me, throwing her hips back and moaning.

Fuck.

I grab my gear and head to the muay thai gym to work out. I need the fucking distraction.

This is going to be really fucking hard.

Puns intended.

Monday morning comes back around and I do what I usually do—I throw myself into work. There's been no contact from Cara since Saturday morning, so it seems like she has the same idea as me. Move on and pretend the whole thing never happened.

"Decker? Is everything okay? I've said your name

three times now," Nadia comments, putting her coffee cup down and staring me. "What's up?"

"Nothing. Sorry, I'm just a little distracted today." Fucking Cara. My life would have been much easier if I'd never met her.

"I can tell. You want to talk about it?" Nadia asks.

I close my laptop and give her my full attention. "Okay, but don't laugh."

"Why would I laugh?"

I press my lips together. "There's a girl."

Her eyes widen.

"And I think I like her—"

"Holy shit, I never thought this day would come." She grins, laughing softly and taking a seat.

My mouth drops indignantly. "You said you wouldn't laugh!"

"I'm sorry, it's just… I've never heard you say something like this before. What usually makes you the happiest is casual sex."

"It was a simpler time," I mutter.

"So what's the problem? Does she not like you back?" Nadia asks, lip twitching.

"I'm never opening up to you again," I deadpan.

"Decker, come on. You haven't been the most…caring with women's feelings, so it's just kind of…karma if you happen to like the one woman who isn't into you."

"It's not that she doesn't like me. She just got out of a long-term relationship, and I actually care about her and don't want to just be a rebound for her," I admit, shrugging. "So I like her, but nothing is going to happen, basically."

"You don't know that. Just because it might not happen right now doesn't mean that it won't happen," she says. "And I truly believe that. I'm not Trade's first love. He didn't think he would love again, but you never know what can happen. And it's nice to know that you can have deeper feelings for a woman. I low-key thought you were broken."

"It's not nice on my end," I grumble, wondering what Cara is doing right now. Did she head home yet? Or is she still at Clover's house? "Caring fucking sucks."

Nadia laughs, shaking her head at me. "It makes you human, Decker. And love is scary, but it's worth it."

I put my hands up. "Okay, who said anything about love?"

She flashes me an amused look and then gets up to go to her desk. Since I became her partner, Nadia redid the office space and our desks are now facing one another.

There is no escaping her now.

"Nice chat," I mutter.

I almost feel worse than before because admitting this shit out loud makes it more real.

I head out to a dodgier part of the neighborhood to follow my client's husband, taking photos for evidence and documenting all of his whereabouts. I knew this was going to be an all-night stakeout, so I prepared with coffee and snacks. My client suspects her husband of cheating on her instead of working late, like he has been telling her. She's already right, he's not at work, but now I just need to take her back the solid evidence of what he truly is up to instead.

Being left alone with my own company though has me wondering if I should text Cara and check in.

Me: Did you get home safely?

I hit send, and then instantly regret my decision. I said I was leaving her alone and here I am reaching out to her first. I do want to make sure she got home safely, though, and that's not a crime. That's being a gentleman, right?

When I see my mark leaving a club with a woman in his arms, leaning over and kissing her, I quickly record a video on my phone. Looks like the wife was right—then again, they usually are. I follow them back to a hotel and watch them disappear inside.

My phone beeps with a message.

Cara: Yeah, about that. I think I'm going to be staying at Clover's for a bit until I sort everything out.

What?
So much for distance going to make this whole thing easier.

Me: Oh really. How come?

Cara: Don't sound too excited lol. Long story, but I think a fresh start is exactly what I need.

Oh shit. I didn't mean to make it sound like I didn't want her to stay in town.

But damn, she just made this whole thing a lot harder

knowing she's just ten minutes away. However, not that I'd admit it out loud, but it feels good to know she is here and not near Rhett.

I groan as my mind goes there.

"You need to stop, Decker," I tell myself.

Me: Just surprised is all. That makes sense, though. What about work?

Cara: The school year just ended. I'll find something new.

Okay, so she really is staying here if she quit her job. No wonder Rhett was calling her, probably wondering where the hell she went. I wonder if she told him she was leaving, or just bailed and left him confused.

Women love doing shit like that.

She texts again.

Cara: What are you doing?

Me: I'm at a stakeout. Cheating husband.

Cara: Bastard

I grin and type back.

Me: How about you?

Cara: I'm babysitting Sapphire so Clover and Felix can have a date night. I thought they'd be back by now, but they are still missing.

Me: Enjoying their freedom.

Cara: Yep! She's fast asleep so I'm just watching TV.

I decide to give her a quick call to hear her voice. "What are you watching?"

"Nothing as exciting as you," she says, amusement in her tone.

"I don't know, I've been sitting here for over an hour," I grumble. "You know what, I can't even remember the last time I had a proper chat on the phone with someone. It's all texting these days."

"Yet here you are, calling me while you're supposed to be working," she teases.

"I can multitask," I reply with a smirk. *Let me show you sometime.*

"Hold on a sec," she says, and I can hear rustling noises and laughter. She puts the phone back to her hear. "Clover and Felix just got home and rushed to their bedroom."

I smirk. "Hope you have some headphones."

She laughs softly. "I don't know, she had grass in her hair—looks like they already did some rolling around."

"Nice to know you can still do shit like that after having a kid," I comment.

"They are proof of that," she says a little dreamily. "Any progress on the cheating husband?"

"Still waiting for him to resurface."

"Tell me about your most exciting case yet…"

We continue to chat until she goes to sleep, and I head home with enough evidence for my client.

Some people you just can't seem to stay away from.

Cara and I could be friends, though. Friends is safe, and I can still be there for her.

Even to myself, I sound like an idiot.

Chapter Sixteen

Cara

After texting Decker all night, I wake up and smile. I don't know why, but picturing him sitting there and following a cheating husband while chatting with me was so amusing. His job definitely sounds interesting, something new every day. I'm sure he never knows where he will end up. I probably should have told him in person that I had decided to stay, but when he asked if I had gotten home safely, I had to let him know.

At first I got the impression he would have preferred me to have left—out of sight out of mind, maybe—and I can understand why. We seem to have some sort of connection, and it's terrifying, and not what we both need right now.

I grab my phone off the nightstand to try to call Rhett back. After he called me when I was at Decker's, I've been trying to reach him but he hasn't been answering the phone, which isn't unusual for him and another reason I'm glad we are over. I'm guessing he wanted to discuss the house, or maybe Dad mentioned I had left. I told him we would still be friends, and I meant it, but being away from him is definitely a good thing for the both of us.

Clover pops her head into my room to see if I'm awake. "Good morning. I made you some coffee."

I sit up in bed as she hands it to me. "Thank you."

"What do you want to do today? I'm going to take Sapphire to the park if you want to join us, and then maybe we could get some lunch," she says, sitting on the edge of my bed.

"Sounds good. I'm going to start applying for jobs today, too."

Clover surprises me by frowning. "Oh man. Can't you take a little time off before you dive back into work? It's so boring being here alone sometimes."

I laugh. "I only have three months before school starts again. Is your daughter boring you, Clover?"

She smirks. "My daughter is wonderful, but having my best friend around every day would be living the dream. An adult I actually like to talk to. Stay-at-home-mom life is hard, okay? I'm looking forward to heading back to work."

Clover has stayed home with Fire long past her maternity leave, with money not being an issue for her. She was promised her job back whenever she chooses to return, but I'll bet she won't last another three months. Clover is very similar to her mother, the infamous Faye Black, who was a lawyer turned FBI agent. She loves the high of closing a case.

"I know it's hard. It's summer, so don't worry, I'm sure you'll have me home with you for a while, but I have to have a look and see what my options are," I say, taking a sip of the caramel-flavored coffee. "I can't crash here forever, Clover. I need a plan."

"Why not?" she asks, completely serious. "You could never outstay your welcome here."

"I know, and I love you for it," I reply, smiling at her. "But I need to decide if I want to stay and get a house here or move back home."

"I think you should stay here," she decides. "Pros: One. I'm here. Two. Fire gets to grow up with her godmother. Three. I'm here. Four. You are away from Rhett and the MC aren't here breathing down your neck. Five. Freedom. And Six. Oh, did I mention that I live here? I also have no friends here, after all of these years, so you should do me a solid and stay here."

"You do so have friends here." I roll my eyes.

"None like you," she replies with a serious face. "And should I also bring up the fact that a certain sexy private investigator lives here too? I always thought he had some big dick energy, and turns out I was right."

I shake my head at my best friend. "I'm not letting a man be a factor in my decision on where I'm going to live."

Clover nods. "Smart. You know I'm here for you no matter what, anything you need."

"I'd be lost without you, Clo."

"No, you wouldn't. You are strong, Cara." She stands up. "Now get dressed. We have a diva to entertain."

She leaves my room and closes the door. I finish my coffee and then send Decker a quick text before getting out of bed and jumping into the shower. He texted first yesterday, so it should be me today.

Me: Good morning.

What the fuck is this man doing to me? I feel like a teenager again.

I hide my phone under the pillow, like that can save me from making any bad decisions, and head for the bathroom.

Change is a weird thing.

It brings out so much in you, good and bad.

I'm just going to have to hold on for the ride.

"Rhett still didn't call you back? He's not answering my calls either," Clover comments as she looks at her phone. After an hour at the park, a shopping trip and a museum, we've settled down for lunch with Sapphire asleep in her stroller.

"Nope. Nothing from him. He's probably knee-deep in women at the clubhouse."

Yeah, the thought does hurt. I'm not completely dead inside, and it does hurt to think of Rhett being with other women. But not as much as it used to hurt when I was still with him. Now, he's not mine. Before, the mere thought of a woman getting his attention used to kill me inside. It's not my problem anymore.

"I'm going to call Dad and see," she says, pressing some buttons and then the phone to her ear. "Hey, Dad. Yes, it's me, your favorite child." She laughs at his reply. "I'm just calling because I've been trying to get a hold of Rhett and I can't. Do you have any idea where he is?" Her brow furrows and her tone changes, now worried. "Is everything all right? Yeah. Okay. Love you too."

She ends the call and looks up at me. "Something is

going on, and Dad doesn't want to tell me. Maybe because it's over the phone, or it's just club business he doesn't want us involved in."

"What did he say?" I ask, confused. Her father, Dex, used to be president of the Wind Dragons but is still very much involved in the club happenings.

"That Rhett has gone away on club business for a few weeks," she replies, crossing her arms. "He said that he is fine, and not to worry. I'll have to try to catch Mom alone—she will probably give me more information."

"The only time members suddenly disappear for a few weeks—"

"Is when some sort of shit is going down," she finishes.

I remember when Rhett and I had to go away once, to keep us safe and away from the drama. That was when we both admitted that we wanted to be together and committed to each other. The beginning of our messed-up, intense love story. This is likely what has happened again, but this time without me. I suddenly feel terrible for missing his call when I was at Decker's house, because he was probably calling to say goodbye and explain what was going on.

"I'm sure he's fine," she says, sensing my worry. She reaches out and takes my hand. "They know what they are doing. He's probably just going to hide out until whatever this is blows over. Although he should have told us what was going down, so we knew. He normally would have."

But everything is different now.

I scrub my hand down my face in frustration. "He tried to call me, and I didn't answer. This is my fault."

"No, it's not. This is the lifestyle that he chose, Cara. He isn't just in the MC, he *is* the MC. They want him to take over when Arrow steps down, which will be soon—he's old now. This is his world, we are just living in it," she says, sighing. "I need to punch something. Times like this I miss the clubhouse. Now I have to go to a boxing gym."

I can tell that she is worried too, but she has no guilt over the situation, unlike me, who dumped Rhett, moved away without telling him and then never answered when he tried to call me.

"I wouldn't mind hitting something," I admit.

"Maybe we should join a muay thai gym," she teases, glancing down at the stroller to check on Sapphire. She's such a chill kid and is so easy to take places.

"Decker is the last thing I need to be worrying about right now," I mutter.

"Yeah, that's why you've been texting him all day." Clover smirks, leaning her elbows on the table, studying me. "You can't fool me, Cara. I know you too well."

"I'm not trying to fool you, more myself because I know that I'm being an idiot," I grumble.

Clover simply shrugs, no judgment on her face. That's just one thing I love about her—she's never quick to judge. Well, with me anyway. "I think you're overthinking it. Do what you want to do. What feels right. Not what you think that you are meant to do. There's nothing wrong with moving on. And Decker is hot as hell. You deserve some of that."

"If I wanted to do what felt right, I'd go over to Decker's right now and have a repeat of the other night. I can't stop thinking about anything else," I blurt out.

She throws her head back and laughs. "That's the power of some good penis. Never underestimate it."

"It's not just that. It's everything about him," I admit quietly. "It's how he makes me feel. I feel safe, I feel comfortable, but still with butterflies in my stomach. He makes me feel sexy, powerful, like I can do anything. It's an addictive feeling."

Her eyes widen, as if only just realizing how much Decker is consuming me so soon. "Okay, I can see why you're worried then. Because it's not just the bomb sex. It's more."

"If I'm being honest with myself, then yeah. The sex wasn't emotionless sex. There was a true connection there. But it's just not the right time; I don't know what I'm supposed to do."

Clover is quiet for a moment before she answers. "Not stress about it is what you're going to do. Just see how it plays out. Enjoy being single again. Enjoy the freedom. Do you want me to break up with Felix for a week or two so I can be wild with you?"

I laugh and roll my eyes at her bad joke. "Okay, I'll take your advice and stop overthinking. I'm going to do what makes me happy."

"And Decker makes you happy?"

I nod.

"Then go for it. You only live once," she says with a cheeky wink.

I smile at her. "Thank you, I think I really needed to hear that."

"I'm here all week," she replies. "Also, three words: Big. Dick. Energy."

We both break down in laughter.
Fire stirs, so we leave the café and head home.
Me with a better mindset than before.

Chapter Seventeen

Decker

The next morning I'm in the office, coffee in hand, when Cara walks inside and glances around.

"Good morning," I say, standing up to greet her.

I'm surprised to see her here, but it's a good surprise. We spent all of yesterday texting, but we hadn't spoken about when we would actually see each other again. I think both of us were being a little more wary about our situation.

At least the sober versions of us are more intelligent, or so I thought. We can't seem to stay away from each other no matter how badly we know that we should.

"Hey," she says, a brown bag in her hand. "I knew you'd already have coffee, so I brought you a bagel."

"Thank you," I say, grinning. "And to what do I owe this bagel and visit?"

Her cheeks flush. "I was in the neighborhood and I wanted to ask you something."

I gesture for her to take a seat, and then sit down opposite her on my chair. "Sure. What's up?"

I pull out the cream cheese and jalapeno bagel and

my mouth starts to water. Can this woman get any better? I don't think that she could.

My door opens once more and Atlas, a member of the Knights of Fury MC, steps in. His eyes go to Cara and then back to me. "Shit, sorry, I'll come back," he says, winking at Cara.

My eyes narrow.

"No, it's okay, come on in," Cara tells him with a friendly smile. "I'm not here on official business."

"Me either." Atlas smirks, walking into my office and making himself welcome.

"Atlas, this is Cara. Cara, Atlas," I introduce, not wanting to be rude, but also not wanting good-looking biker Atlas to look at Cara ever again.

Cara eyes his leather cut and nods. "Nice to meet you."

I never thought about her allegiance with the Wind Dragons MC, and how that might affect how she sees other clubs. Are the Wind Dragons friends with the Knights?

"You too," he says, then looks over at me with much less enthusiasm. "Temper asked me to drop this off to you." He pulls out an envelope from his jeans pocket and hands it over to me.

"Thanks," I say, scanning what looks like an invitation. Someone must be getting married.

"See ya," he says to the two of us, and then leaves.

Cara brings those inquisitive brown eyes to me. "So hanging out with my family wasn't the first time you've hung out with bikers, huh?"

I grin. "Something like that. You heard of the Knights of Fury MC before?"

She shakes her head. "Nope. The only other clubs I hear about are the ones that I have to avoid because they will try to kidnap me and use me against the Wind Dragons."

My eyes widen. "Seriously?"

She nods, wincing. "I'm afraid so. There are times we have to go into a lockdown and all stay together, because if they know who we are, the other club will use us against our parents."

"And this was just your life growing up?" I ask, wondering what that must have been like. It's definitely not a normal upbringing. No wonder she's so different from all the other women I have met.

"Yeah, I mean, not all the time. Most of the time it was just a normal childhood, but we were all trained from a young age so we could defend ourselves. When shit hit the fan, we had to all look over our shoulders, and would sometimes have members of the MC escorting us everywhere so we would be safe," she explains, giving me an insight into her world.

"Would you want your kids to grow up like that?" I ask, curious.

"No. I mean, there are some aspects that I would use with my own children—like I'd like them to be capable and learn self-defense, and all of that. But I'd like a more quiet life for them, I think. And one where I would never have to worry about their safety. Probably impossible for someone like me, but a girl can dream. How about you? What was your childhood like?"

"It was good," I say. "My mom was a nurse, so she worked hard and we were often left to fend for ourselves, but we always had everything that we needed and were always well loved. My dad walked out on us when I was about ten, so it was just me, my mom and my baby sister, Simone. My mom died a few years ago, so it's just me and my sister now. We are really close. She owns a dog-grooming business not far from here."

"I'm sorry that you lost your mom," she replies, reaching out and touching my hand. "She sounds like an amazing woman."

"She was. Some people say a woman can't raise a man, but she did just that with me." I clear my throat, getting emotional just thinking about her. "I think you and Simone would get on like a house on fire."

She smiles. "That's good to know. I'd love to meet her."

Fuck. Now we're talking about meeting family.

But we're friends, right? And friends do that shit all the time.

"Felix was telling me about some memories about when you two were partners. Did you not like being a cop?" she asks, leaning her cheek on the inside of her palm and staring up at me.

She never looked so beautiful.

"I did love being a cop at the time, but once I became friends with the Knights of Fury MC, the lines started becoming a little blurred and people noticed. But to be honest, I was tired of watching criminals walk away on technicalities. I'm aware there's nothing I could do about it, but knowing a murderer would just be let go for nothing other than an administrative error started to get to me. It was just the change I really needed," I explain. "I also felt a lot of frustration over being reprimanded for finding true justice for a murder. There's a lot to it, but I feel right about my decision."

She looks pensive before replying. "I mean, no dis-respect, but how does becoming a private investigator change that? Or are you running around in a bat suit acting as a vigilante?"

A laugh bursts out of me. This woman gets me. "I wish I could have all the cool gadgets Batman has, and the idea of chasing bad guys is a fun one. But no, I'm under no illusions—now I get paid to find evidence of cheating spouses and I'm not doing anything to help the problem. I just… I at least know what I'm getting into with the PI work. It's like all the best parts of being a cop without the paperwork and political BS. And I still help put bad people away. It's not just chasing in-fidelities."

"I get it." She looks around the office. "This place is pretty cool. And it would be an interesting job. And yeah, the biker ties wouldn't affect you here. How close are you to the Knights?"

"I know the Knights through Nadia," I explain. "Nadia is engaged to Trade, who is the brother of the Knights' president, Temper. I'm on good terms with them all and consider them friends." I realize I don't quite know the etiquette or rules about MCs and whether she's allowed to associate with me since I am friends with the Knights. I'm assuming she is or else she would've said something.

"Good to know you aren't opposed to some biker ties. It's definitely a biker-friendly zone here. Even if you are a Wind Dragon." I give her a wink.

She laughs. "Wonderful," she replies, lip twitching. "So, I actually did come in here for a reason…"

"That's right, you did."

"I was going to ask Felix to help me with this, but work is hectic for him right now and I felt bad asking. I want to trade in my car and get a new one. I was wondering if you knew anything about cars. I just need someone to come in with me who knows what they are talking about so the car dealer doesn't take advantage of my lack of knowledge."

She rushes the words out like she hates asking for help, and knowing her personality, I imagine that she does. I want her to feel comfortable asking me for help when she needs it, so I make sure to answer her gently.

"Of course, I'd love to help. And yeah, I know a thing or two about cars," I say, smiling widely at her. "When do you want to go?"

"Thank you so much. Whenever you are free. I'd normally have my dad for all of this stuff…" She glances up at me through her lashes, a sheepish look dashing across her face. "I probably sound spoiled, don't I? I promise you that I'm an otherwise capable adult—"

"Cara, it's fine. I have a sister, and I do all of this kind of stuff with her. Like I said, I'm more than happy to help you with whatever you need," I say.

"Thank you."

"You're welcome. So what new car do you want? You got sick of the Mercedes?" I ask.

She shrugs and tucks her hair behind her ear. "I loved it, but I think I just want something new. I need a change, and I'm starting with getting rid of Mercy the Mercedes."

"Mercy? Original," I tease.

"I have my eye on an Audi," she replies, pulling her

phone out and showing me a picture. "What do you think?"

"It's nice," I say, nodding in approval. "How about tomorrow morning at eight? My first client is in at ten a.m."

"Sounds perfect, thank you," she says, leaning over the desk to kiss me on the cheek. "I'll see you tomorrow."

"Yep," I call out, touching my cheek where her lips just left.

I need to admit to myself that Cara is now a part of my life, and I do care about her.

I just hope she's ready for this.

Chapter Eighteen

Cara

I meet Decker at his office the next morning, and then we leave together for the car dealership. I'm going to be sad to say goodbye to Mercy, but I'd like a fresh start with everything, including my vehicle. I have too many memories of me and Rhett in the backseat, times when we couldn't wait to go home to have each other, so we just parked at the beach and got naked in the back. Us being young, reckless and in love. I'm not the same person I was back then, and I want a new car to make new memories in, as stupid as it might sound to others.

I'm glad Decker said he would come with me, because I didn't want to come alone. Clover would come with me, and she might have a big mouth on her, but she doesn't know much about cars. I could have asked Felix—though I meant what I said, he's been really busy with work—but the real reason is I just want Decker to be here.

And I'm happy he is.

This time he had a coffee and a bagel waiting for me, which I thought was really cute.

"So this is the one?" he asks, stopping to stand next to the black Audi. "Black is obviously your favorite color."

I touch the hood of the car. "Yeah, look how good it looks."

We have a proper look at the car. Decker checks the engine and a few other things I have no idea about.

"It looks good. I think we should get a mechanic to come in and have a look at it first, since it's preowned, but to me she looks pretty perfect," he says, giving his approval. "And you are going to look hot as fuck in it."

Our eyes connect and hold for a second, before he looks back at the car. I find myself wanting him to look back at me, but instead I smile and reply with, "Good to know."

Decker calls up a mechanic he knows and asks him to come in and check out the car. At least, I thought it was a him—until a beautiful woman appears, hugging Decker like she knows him really well.

Did he call someone he has slept with to come and look at my new car? What the hell?

"Cara, this is Demi, the best mechanic in town," he introduces.

Demi, with her dark hair and big blue eyes, offers me one of her tatted hands. She is covered in tattoos, even having one on her neck and a little star at the corner of her pretty right eye. "Nice to meet you, Cara. Now let's have a look at this baby and make sure she is all ready to go for you."

"Thank you," I say to her, moving next to Decker as he watches her work. I clear my throat. "So how do you know her?"

I try to keep my tone even and passive, because I'm not his girlfriend and he can be around whoever he likes. Also, people are allowed to be friends with their exes, just like me and Rhett are. It would be hypocritical of me to have a problem with that.

Then why am I feeling this way?

I feel...jealous.

HE ISN'T EVEN MINE.

But he could be.

"Demi? She's my sister's best friend, so we grew up together. She really is good at what she does, though. Trust me," he says, our shoulders touching.

Sister's friend.

He doesn't mention whether they have ever been more than friends, and I don't ask because it's none of my damn business.

"You okay?" he asks when I go quiet.

I nod and force a smile. "Yeah, I'm fine. Just deciding on what to call the car if she passes the check."

He laughs. "And? What are you thinking?"

"Ari the Audi has a certain ring to it."

Demi looks over and watches Decker laughing. In that moment, I know, as a woman, that even if she hasn't had him, at some point she sure as hell has wanted him. You don't look at a man that way unless you want him.

She closes the door and comes over to us. "You're right, Decker, she's good to go. Previous owners have taken good care of it."

"Thanks, Demi," he says, glancing over at me excitedly. "You got a new car. Fresh start, right?"

I nod. "Exactly."

We sort out all the paperwork and leave in the new car, Mercy and all of her memories staying behind.

Decker hooks up my Bluetooth from my phone, so I can listen to my playlists in the car. Kyla Imani's "Trackstar" plays from the speakers, her smooth voice filling the space. I park in front of his office, and turn to face him. "Thank you for coming with me. Can you tell Demi to send me an invoice for checking the car?"

"I've got it covered, don't worry about it," he says, undoing his seat belt.

"Decker, don't be silly."

"It's nothing, Cara."

He reminds me of the men I grew up with. They never let their women pay for anything. It took a while for me to understand that it wasn't a sign of ownership or making their women indebted to them. It was about showing their women that they wanted to provide and care for them.

I purse my lips. "Okay. I'm bringing you lunch on your break today, then."

It doesn't cover it, but at least I can feed him. Food is love.

He reaches out and cups my face. "You don't have to do that."

"I want to."

"Okay." He grins, scanning my eyes and caressing my jaw with his thumb. "You are so beautiful, you know that?"

For some reason I decide that this is the perfect time to blurt out, "Have you and Demi…"

His eyes widen in surprise. "No, we haven't. Just friends."

"So you're saying she's never tried to hook up with you?" I ask, not believing it for one second.

I'm a woman.

I know.

"She expressed interest once, a long time ago. But I knew my sister wouldn't like that, so I let her down gently. She hasn't brought it up since, we've just all been friends," he admits, eyes lowering to my lips. "If I wanted her, I'd have had her."

"You're such an arrogant..." I trail off, our eyes locked and holding.

"Yes?"

"You know what you are."

His lips kick up at the corners in a sexy smirk.

The tension in the car starts to thicken and all I want is for him to kiss me. I look down at his lips, and then back up at him.

I know he's thinking about it, because his eyes are also on my lips. I'd love to know what is running through his mind right now.

He doesn't make the first move, so I do. I press my lips against his and kiss him sweetly, slowly, until he takes over and deepens the kiss, his hand moving to the back of my neck to take control. I sigh in contentment against him. The kiss feels so right; the chemistry I feel with him is insane, tingles shooting all through my body.

He pulls back and studies me, scanning my eyes. "Are you sure?" he asks, his tone deep and husky.

I nod. "I'm so fucking sure."

He kisses me again, as if proving his point.

When we pull away, I'm breathless, panting, and turned on like I've never been before.

"I have to go back to work," he murmurs, kissing me once again and then on my forehead. He opens the car door and then closes it. "I'm going to need a minute."

I look down at his crotch and see his hard cock pressing against his pants.

Fuck.

He drives me fucking crazy.

A few more moments and a kiss on the cheek, then he's off.

When lunchtime comes around, I pick up some Italian food and drop it off to him. He's busy at his desk when I arrive.

"Food is here," I say, placing the bag on the desk.

"Thank you, Cara. Saves me from running out," he says, putting his pen down and relaxing in his chair. He studies me and smiles. "I haven't stopped thinking about you. You going to stay and eat with me?"

I shake my head. "No, I have to go meet Clover and Sapphire. I just wanted to feed you to say thank you."

"Thank *you*."

Unable to help myself, I walk over to his side of the desk and sit down in front of him. His hand lands on my thigh and he glances over at the door, as if anticipating someone to walk in. We share a quick, sneaky kiss, and he growls when I step away from him.

I wave and take my leave.

I meet up with Clover at the park, where she has planned a picnic for the three of us.

My jaw drops when I see just how extra this picnic

is, with pillows laid out on the grass and a picnic rug covered in crackers, cheeses, fruit and cold meat.

"Why is this one of the most romantic things anyone has done for me?" I ask, sitting down and picking up a green grape.

Clover laughs and gestures to the dips. "I even got your favorite hummus with jalapenos."

"I can see that. And this is why you are one hundred percent my soul mate."

Sapphire comes over to me and sits on my lap. "You have a wonderful mama, you know that, Fire?" She grins.

"She knows," Clover boasts, opening the dip lid and studying me. "How did it go with Decker?"

"I just dropped the food off and we kissed. Again," I blurt out.

"What? Finally!"

"I know. I think he was waiting for me to be ready. To be sure."

"So are you two friends with benefits now? Is that what's going on here?" she asks, arching her brow.

"I have no idea what is going on here," I admit in a dry tone. I kiss the top of Sapphire's hair. "But I think I realized something today."

"And what's that?"

"I think I like him more than he likes me." I wince. "I mean, I kissed him first. He had such good control, and I don't like it."

Clover's eyes widen. "Bull—" She looks down at Fire. "He definitely wants you. You are under his skin just as much, or even more, than he is under yours. He just has a better poker face. He's more experienced than you, Cara. You've only been with Rhett. From what Felix has told me Decker has"—she mouths *slept* and then continues—"with everyone in the whole city. If this is a game, he is a pro."

I grit my teeth at her description. "This isn't a game, though. And I don't get the feeling that he's treating it as such. I think we both just genuinely have no idea what we are doing. Or we do, and know that it's not right."

The ultimate battle of mind versus heart.

"Maybe he's trying to follow your lead. You are the one who just got out of a serious relationship. Maybe he doesn't want to be your rebound." Clover shrugs and I realize that could be true. He has held back and I can see from his perspective why he'd wait for me to make the first move. Huh.

"I think you may be right."

"Life is always a game," Clover responds, picking up a cracker and handing it to Sapphire. "There are winners and there are losers. It just depends on what you want out of it, and what your end goal is."

"I want him."

"Nice to hear you admit that. Any news from Con?"

"We've been texting. I know you don't like her, Clover, but you need to give her a chance," I say.

Clover purses her lips. "It's not that I don't like her. I just want you to be careful. I don't want her to take advantage of you. You give so much, Cara. And if Con is a taker, I know that you will give her anything she wants because she's your sister. If today she messaged and asked for money, you'd ask how much, wouldn't you?"

She's right, I probably would, but wouldn't anyone want to help someone in need?

I glance over to the parking lot, where I notice a man sitting in a black car watching us a little too closely. "Don't look now, but there's someone watching us."

"Black car?"

I nod.

"I saw him pull in when you did."

"You think he's following us?"

"I don't know," she admits, looking down at Fire. "But we should get out of here, just in case. Do you want to ride with us?"

"No, I'll be okay. I'll follow you."

I only just got this car, and I'm not going to leave it behind. This might be nothing, and it will only take me an extra few minutes anyway.

I wait until Fire is safe in the car, then I quickly go to my own. As soon as I open the car door, a van rushes into the parking lot and two men get out.

Fuck.

A second later, they are on me and I'm fighting for my life.

Chapter Nineteen

Decker

When Felix calls and tells me to come to his house, I head there straight away. He rarely demands things from me so I know something is wrong. The door opens just as I lift my hand to knock.

Felix opens the door wide, and I see Cara and Clover huddled together on the couch. "What happened?"

He closes the door and leads me over to them. Cara lifts her face up to me and her eyes are red, like she's been crying. "Felix, I told you not to call him."

"Why wouldn't I? I need his help," Felix chides, turning to me. "Okay, so today, Cara was walking back to her car and someone tried to kidnap her by pulling her into their van. She was lucky—fought the guys off and ran."

"What? Are you okay?" I ask, giving her a quick once-over before sitting next to her.

"I'm fine, just a little shaken is all. I think, being away from the Wind Dragons, I kind of lowered my guard a little when I really shouldn't have," she replies, as I reach for her hand to comfort her. "I should know better, always stay alert."

"You got away, that's all that matters," I say, then glance back up at Felix. "Whatever you need me to do, I'm here."

"Decker, you don't have to—"

"We thought you might say that," Clover says, cutting her off and speaking to me. "We also think we know what's going on, but we haven't called the Wind Dragons yet to confirm."

"What do you think the reason is?" I ask, giving Cara's hand a squeeze.

"We were told Rhett was sent away because something went down in the MC. We don't know what because they didn't tell us, but it has to be connected. Cara must be targeted because of Rhett. No one other than our close friends and family know that they broke up. Both of their names are on their house and their mail, et cetera. I think whatever is going on with Rhett is now touching Cara. Someone wants revenge and they came here to get it."

"But you have no idea what situation Rhett is in?" I ask, brow furrowing.

I don't like this one bit. Why is Rhett's shit touching Cara, and why isn't the MC on top of this? Maybe they thought she'd be safe since she's also out of town, but apparently not.

"Nope. I called my dad, but I'm waiting for him to call back," Cara explains, shrugging. "I know he's going to tell me to come home, which I don't want to do, but I don't want to put any of you in danger either."

"Is going home safer, though?" Clover asks her, frowning. "They'd have you locked up in the clubhouse, and who knows how long this will take to blow over.

We just need to know what Rhett has got himself into before we make a plan. We don't even know who or what we are up against."

Cara nods. "You're right."

Cara's phone rings and she puts her father on speakerphone. "Hey, Dad. Where have you been? I've been calling you for the last hour."

"Sorry, Cara, some shit was going down here. Are you okay?"

"Yeah, I'm okay, but something has happened. I was walking back to my car after leaving the park today and a van pulled up and some men tried to kidnap me. We think it has something to do with my connection to Rhett."

"Fuck," he grits out, adding a few more curse words for good measure. "I'm so sorry, honey. I didn't realize they'd dig this deep. I'm going to come there now. I'll explain everything. Don't go anywhere alone."

"Okay, I'll see you soon."

We all share a look.

Clover stands. "I'll go check on Fire and then make us some coffee." Felix follows behind her, leaving me and Cara alone.

She leans her head against my shoulder and I pull her into my arms, like I've been wanting to do this entire time.

"I'm so glad you are okay," I whisper.

"I told you what my life can be like," she sighs, shielding those beautiful brown eyes from me. "Thank you for coming and offering your help. You know I didn't expect you to."

"Cara, of course I'd come if any of you needed me,"

I say, swallowing hard. "But I would especially be there for you. Whenever."

She lifts her head and smiles at me. "I wish I could say this is the first time that someone has tried to kidnap me, but it's not."

"Lucky you're a pro escape artist then," I tease, holding on to her tightly. "I wish the Wind Dragons would have given you more information so that we know how to keep you safe."

"Me too. They must have one hundred percent thought it wouldn't touch me since I wasn't in town anymore. Whatever it is, this gang must really want to get back at the MC if they are going through all of this effort."

Clover returns with coffee. "Mom just called, she said she's on her way, too. There goes the neighborhood."

Cara smiles. She is obviously well loved by her friends and family, and I hope she knows that.

We're on our second cup of coffee when Cara's parents arrive about two hours later. Rake rushes in and hugs her tightly, and I can see how relieved he is that she is okay. The same with Bailey, who rubs her back and closes her eyes.

"I am so sorry, Cara," Rake says, shaking his head. "We had no idea that they would try something like this. We underestimated them. And it won't happen again."

Rake looks over at me and nods, while Bailey sits next to me. "Nice to see you again, Decker."

"You too. I wish it was under better circumstances."

"You and me both," she says.

After everyone greets one another, we all sit down and get to the bottom of this.

"Who did you underestimate?" Felix asks, getting straight to the point. "We need to know what we are up against here."

Rake nods, glancing around the room. His eyes land on me. "We trust him?"

A chorus of agreements echo around the room. My favorite has to be the yes that easily slips from Cara's sweet lips.

"Okay," he replies, stretching his jean-clad legs out. "There's a new street gang in our neighborhood. And not just a bunch of young kids getting into shit—these men are dangerous. They deal drugs and have the numbers to cause some trouble."

"So what happened that Rhett had to leave?" Cara asks.

"Arrow and Rhett went to speak to the gang members about selling drugs on our territory. We wanted to keep the peace, but let them know where we stand, too. Unfortunately, Rhett got caught in the middle of a gang war. Guns were pulled and Rhett accidentally injured a young boy while protecting himself, which happened to be one of the gang leaders' sons."

I wince at what I'm hearing. Regardless of it being an accident, hearing about a boy being hurt is never a good thing.

"Despite this not being an MC issue, because Rhett was the one who injured the boy, his life is now in danger and they want blood," Rake explains, clenching and unclenching his fists. "We thought the best thing to do would be to send him away until we can sort it out, because they said they want him dead. Never once did we think they would find Cara. Hell, they broke up and she moved away, so we thought she was safe."

"How injured was the boy?" Clover asks.

"I'm not sure exactly, but we know he was shot in the leg. He's alive, I do know that," Rake says, looking over at Cara. "My first reaction is to take you home with me, but with the rest of the gang there, that doesn't make sense either."

"Now that we know what's going on, we can protect Cara from here," I say to her dad, sharing a look with Felix, who nods his agreement. "We have me, Felix, Clover and my friends that could help us."

Rake arches a brow. "You mean the Knights of Fury MC?"

I nod. "If needed."

"The Wind Dragons look after their own," he states.

Bailey rolls her eyes. "Now is not the time for you to be proud, Rake. Our daughter is in danger, and I don't care if we have to pull in a favor with the devil himself if that's what's going to keep her safe."

"The Wind Dragons have no beef with the Knights," Clover says to Rake, shrugging. "I don't see why uniting in this would be a bad thing. This is Knights territory, so they should know what is going on. Like you said, the gang has numbers. With the Knights at our backs, so do we."

Rake hesitantly agrees. "Okay, Decker. You give me a contact from the Knights and I will speak to them."

I nod.

Now I just have to hope that Temper will agree to helping us.

Shit. What am I pulling the Knights into?

Chapter Twenty

Cara

Watching Decker stand up to my dad, telling him that he can protect me if I stay here, has me wanting to jump his bones right here and now. I don't want to go back home—it would feel like a step backwards even if it was just until this all died down.

I have to admit that this is not how I thought my day would go. I shudder as I remember the van pulling up and two men running out, with the third driving. They were dressed in black and had ski masks covering their faces, so even security footage wouldn't show who they were.

One grabbed me from behind while the other tried to pick me up and drag me into the black van. I managed to elbow the one behind me, fight them off, and then I got into my car and drove off. I was shaken up. I just wasn't expecting anything to happen to me in a town where no one knew me. Just proves that no place is safe—I'll forever be looking over my shoulder for the rest of my life. I should have listened to Clover and got into her car, but that might have put her and Fire in danger, so it's probably a good thing that I didn't.

"You okay?" Decker asks me.

I nod. "Yeah, I will be. I'm still taking all of this in."

Especially about Rhett. I still feel bad I didn't answer his call. He must have felt so guilty hurting that young boy, but he *should* feel that way. An innocent kid shouldn't be caught in the middle of all this bullshit, no matter who his father is.

Faye and Sin arrive, and Faye rushes over to me to pull me into her arms. "I'm so glad you're okay, Cara. And I'm so sorry this happened to you. Everyone wanted to come and see you but hello, someone has to man the clubhouse. But they all send their love."

Clover joins us in a big hug. "She's going to stay here with us."

Faye touches her daughter's hair. "I think that's for the best—it would be worse at home. I'm assuming you are well prepared for such events, Clover?"

Clover grins, flashing her teeth. "Let's just say anyone who tries to come here won't be leaving alive."

"Wonderful. Now where is my granddaughter?" she asks, heading for Fire's room.

"She's asleep!" Clover calls out, following behind her. "If you break it, you bought it!"

Sin approaches and gives me a warm hug. "Fought off two grown men, huh? I'm pleased to see you are still in fine form."

"Me too." I grin. "Lucky we were raised to survive."

"I'm sorry, we should have known better. Prez is pissed and wanted to be here, but I'm sure you can imagine the damage control he's trying to pull right now."

I nod. "It's okay. I'm just happy to know what is going on and why I was targeted."

I know that while technically Rhett is to blame, this is just part of being close with the Wind Dragons. There are so many positives, but there are always times like this when our lives are in danger. I sometimes wonder what it's like for normal people who don't have to worry about anything like this in their day-to-day lives. I suppose crime can happen to anyone, but with me I know it's always personal.

And it always sucks.

Until this is over, I won't have any freedom to go anywhere alone and I'm going to have to avoid going to places where I can't be easily protected. It's probably for the best that I haven't gotten a summer school job, because that would make all of this much harder.

"We'll put our house in full security mode," Felix says as he comes over, putting his arm around me. "I have to admit that we've gotten a little lax with nothing happening for a long time, but we will use the security gate and I'll set the alarms up. Everything. The cameras have always been in use, and they are connected to my and Clover's phones. So even if we aren't here, we can still see everything. I'm a cop and Clover is FBI; if anyone can pull this off, it's us."

"I'm sorry that I brought this to your home, Felix."

He waves off my apology like it's no big deal. "It comes with the territory. And we've set up our house with these kinds of situations in mind. One word and we're becoming Fort Knox."

"You guys are the best."

I truly have the best friends and family in the world,

and that's what balances out the negatives of being in this lifestyle.

And Decker.

I look over to find him talking to my mom and dad. I can tell that Mom likes him, but my dad is a little unsure. And fair enough too—Rhett is a member of the MC and has known Dad since he was a kid.

Decker is a stranger.

But that doesn't mean that he's not better for me. Character is more important than how long you have known someone. Someone you have just met can have better intentions for you than someone you have known forever.

Faye comes out into the living room holding Fire and kissing her cheeks. "Look who woke up!"

Clover looks at me and shakes her head, and I can't help but laugh. It sucks that this is what brought us all here together, but at the same time it's really nice to have them here.

"I'll get some wine," Clover declares, and I walk with her into the kitchen. "Do you think wine will cut it? Or do you need something a little stronger?"

"Wine is fine," I reply, amused.

"Decker fits in well with the family," she absently comments as she reaches up to get some glasses. "Do you think your dad is telling him to not let you out of his sight?"

"I have no doubt. I feel bad that this is being put on him. I told Felix and you not to involve him."

"As if he wouldn't have found out. And then he would have been pissed that he didn't know," she says, flashing me a knowing look. "Admit it. And he wants to help, so let the man help. I don't think you could even stop him if we tried. He obviously cares about you a lot, Cara."

"I know."

It's just not the ideal situation when you like a guy. I'm a proud, independent woman, and I don't love asking for or needing someone's help. But Clover is right. I don't think we could get him to walk away if we wanted him to. He's here because he cares not just about me, but about all of us. I never once in my life thought I would find myself in a situation where Rhett wouldn't be the one protecting me. Instead, Rhett's the one who has gotten me into shit and Decker is the one helping me out.

It's funny how life can change so quickly.

Clover pulls out two trays and places all the filled wineglasses on them like we're at some fancy party. "Help me take these out. Then I'll make a platter for everyone."

I take one of the trays. "I love you, you know that, right?"

"Of course I do," she replies. "No gang is going to take us out, don't even worry about it. And guess what?"

"What?"

"Looks like I got my wish after all… You are stuck hanging out with me and Fire until this all dies down." She laughs, evilly.

And I can't help but laugh along with her.

Laugh or cry, right?

"Can I interest you in some wine to make light of the need for this gathering?" I ask Decker, who is now standing alone with my mom.

"No thank you, I'd like to stay alert just in case,"

he replies, smirking. "But I'm sure this beautiful lady here will have one."

"I will," Mom replies, taking a glass and having a quick sip. "I like him."

I roll my eyes at him buttering her up and her absolutely loving it, and then walk away to offer everyone else a drink.

Dad, like Decker, declines the offer. "What's going on with you two? You and Rhett only just broke up. Do you think it's a good idea to get involved with someone so soon? Especially an ex-cop."

"We aren't together, Dad," I say. His words mirror my own thoughts—well, not the ex-cop part, but the fact that I'm only recently single. "He's a friend."

"I wasn't born yesterday, Cara. Why do you think he's here doing anything he can to protect you? You two haven't known each other that long. It's not that I don't like him—he seems like a good man—but that doesn't mean that you should move on so quickly," he says, eyes scanning mine.

I pick up one of the wineglasses and take a big gulp. "I know, Dad. And I know that he likes me, and yeah, I like him. But like I said, we are just friends."

He nods slowly. "I know that in the end Rhett wasn't always good for you, but he does love you still. It would hurt him to see you move on so fast."

I finish the rest of the wine and put the empty glass back on the tray, gritting my teeth. "I love Rhett, but he wasn't thinking about me when he was sleeping with other women, so I don't think I need to consider his feelings right now, just my own."

If Rhett were any other man, what's the bet Dad

would have kicked his face in? But this is the golden child and future leader of the MC. I'm sure Dad spoke to him, but the man is still standing, which would be a different story if someone who wasn't a member of the Wind Dragons treated me in that way.

Double standards?

Yeah, I fucking think so.

"I love you, but I'm an adult and I'm in a weird place right now, not to mention everything else going on, so I need to find my way on my own. And if that leads me to Decker or not, that is my decision," I say to Dad.

He sighs and pulls me into his arms. "I worry about you. And so do your mom and your sister. She wanted to come but couldn't get off work tomorrow."

"I know; she messaged me. Do you think they will try to come after her?"

"I don't know, but we're taking all precautions. She's safe and not going anywhere alone."

Mom comes up and wraps her arms around me from behind. "I can stay here with you if you like, Cara. Dad has to go back, but I can be here if you need me."

"Mom, I'm fine," I assure her. "I have an army around me. And you both need to make sure Natalie is okay, and yourselves."

I know she hates to be without my dad, and I wouldn't do that to her. Plus, what can she really do? Follow me around so I'm not alone, too? I don't want to put her in any danger—she's safer with the MC.

Faye comes over to stand with us, her long hair curtained around her beautiful face. "This feels just like old times, don't you think? Nothing brings family together like someone almost being kidnapped."

When you spend time with Faye, you get to know exactly why Clover is how she is.

She turns to me, her eyes gentling. Faye has always loved me like another daughter and I've always loved her like my second mother. "You know, now that you're available again—Asher is always single."

I laugh. Asher is Clover's younger brother who joined the army, so it's far and few between when we get to see him. "Asher is like my brother, but thank you for the approval."

She looks over at Decker, who is holding Fire, smiling down at her as she giggles in his arms.

My ovaries explode.

"Okay, I stand by your choice," she mutters, eyes going wide.

Dad growls at her. "Don't encourage her, Faye."

I love the relationship they all have. It's just how I picture all of us to be when we are older. Close and all up in each other's business. They know each other so well and have been through so much together. The loyalty is strong.

"Rake, she is a grown woman," Faye says back to him, rolling her eyes. "And not all men are how you were."

Mom smirks at that dig. "Even the worst of the players can be reformed."

I wrinkle my nose. I really don't know if I want to be hearing this conversation.

"I think you are all getting ahead of yourself—"

"I tried to get some gossip out of Felix," Faye admits, whispering now. "But he wouldn't give me anything.

He's loyal to Decker, and that is a good sign. I have no doubt he has some miles on him, though."

I choke on my second glass of wine, and Faye taps me on the back. Decker comes over, Fire still in his arms. "Are you okay?"

"I'm fine," I say, clearing my throat. "Just drank my wine a little too quickly."

Fire reaches out for me and I take her from Decker. He watches me with her and the look in his eyes, I don't know if I like it.

It's probably the same look I had just before when he was holding her.

We are both so fucked.

Chapter Twenty-One

Decker

While everyone settles in to stay the night here and head home in the morning, I go back to my house alone. It's a little sad, to be honest. I find myself missing being around all of that warmth instantly. Not to mention Cara looked pretty good with a kid on her hip, like she was born to be a mother. I liked seeing her like that—probably a little too much. I get a text from her as soon as I get inside.

Cara: Thank you so much for everything today.

Me: No need to thank me.

After I text Cara back, I send a message to Simone to make sure she got home safely, and then to Nadia. I tell her that I will finish up the cases I'm working on, but after that I'm going to need to take a week or so off to help a friend. She calls me instantly, and I tell her everything that is going on.

"This is the girl you were telling me about, isn't it?" she asks afterward.

"That obvious?"

She laughs. "Take as long as you need, that's fine. I can postpone any clients that contact us. And I will set up a meeting with you and Temper, if you like. I think the Knights will definitely help you."

"With your pressure, you mean?"

She laughs quietly again. "With Trade's, no doubt. Temper would never say no to his brother."

"I owe you one."

"You owe me nothing, Decker. It's nothing you wouldn't do for any of us."

We end the call and I jump in the shower, processing everything that happened tonight. I still can't believe that we almost lost Cara today. Who knows what they would have done to her? I'm not going to lie; the thought scares me to my core and puts everything into perspective for me. Who gives a fuck if in theory now is not the right time for us?

I don't want to sit there idly, waiting for the right time.

What if that time never comes?

What if she meets someone else, or decides to go back to Rhett?

I'm not going to let that happen.

I don't want to waste any more time pretending that I don't want her, and that I'm not crazy about her.

I am.

And I want her to be mine.

Every minute we aren't together is a waste of time.

I just need her to see it now.

* * *

The next morning, I step into the Knights of Fury club-house and the first person I see is Crow.

"You joining the MC now or what?" he asks, grinning as he offers me a handshake.

"You wish. Temper around? He's expecting me."

"Of course he is, or you wouldn't have made it through that gate," he replies, smirking. "He's sitting out in the back."

"Thanks."

I head outside and see Temper sitting there with a coffee, typing something on his phone. He looks up when he hears the slide door opening.

"Hey, thanks for seeing me."

"Trade already gave me a rundown on your situation," he says, getting straight to business. Temper is not a man whose bad side I'd ever want to be on. He has something about him, something that makes me aware he could be very dangerous if he needed to. "I didn't know that you knew any of the Wind Dragons."

Lucky for me, he's on the same side.

"Well, I didn't," I admit, sitting down next to him. "My ex-partner is married to a member's daughter—"

"And you are pussy-whipped by Rake's daughter," he cuts me off, lip twitching. "This tie to the Wind Dragons could be a good thing. They are a strong MC. Good men."

I should have known he would look at it from a club perspective. I don't care what gets him there, though, I just need his agreement to help Cara by giving us the extra manpower if it becomes necessary.

"They are," I agree.

"Tell me what you want from us."

"I want you to have our backs if shit goes down, and it might. And I want your men to help us protect her, in whatever way possible."

He nods once. "All right. You can have Atlas, Aries and Diesel to protect her. And if shit goes down, you have all of us. Just keep me updated. And I want as much information as you have on this gang. I've heard about them, and I don't want them coming here," he says, brown eyes on me.

"Yes, and thank you," I say.

"If Arrow wants to speak to me, give him my number."

"I will."

I leave the clubhouse feeling much better, knowing that we now have an unstoppable team at Cara's back.

They tried to kidnap the wrong woman.

I drive straight from the clubhouse to see Cara, their gate now firmly closed. I text her to let me in, and the gates open a minute later. She comes outside to wait for me to get out of my car, and greets me with a hug. She's all dressed up, in a long black cotton dress with sandals. Her hair is up in a bun on top of her head, her brown eyes lined in black.

"Hey." She smiles. "You just missed everyone."

"They drove back?" I ask as I close the car door.

She nods. "We all went out for breakfast and then they left."

"Breakfast? Is it safe for you to be leaving the house?"

I'm not sure why she looks amused. "There was a group of us and I don't know if you know this, but my dad is kind of badass."

"Right," I mutter.

"Have you eaten yet?"

"Yes, I grabbed something on the way. Felix is at work?" I ask as I follow her inside.

"Yeah, Felix went to work, but he's trying to organize some time off. Clover is putting Fire down for a nap—she didn't sleep well last night."

"I just went to the Knights' clubhouse," I say, leaning against the kitchen counter while she starts to make some coffee for both of us.

Cara pauses. "What did they say?"

"They said they will help us with whatever we need. Three men to help us protect you and the rest of the men, if needed. Temper said Arrow is welcome to contact him whenever if he wishes to discuss," I explain, sitting down on a barstool.

"So that means I definitely won't have to go back home." She smiles widely and comes over to give me another hug, this one lingering, her hand never leaving my arm. "Thank you, Decker."

"Don't thank me. It's my friend Nadia they are really doing this for," I admit, reaching out and touching her cheek. I want to kiss her so badly.

"I'd like to meet her then," she replies, gaze dropping to my lips. "To say thank you."

"I'm sure I can organize that."

I lean forward and press my lips against hers, testing at first, to see if she pulls away or tells me that this is a bad idea, but she doesn't.

She closes the space between us, melting into the kiss, and moves to straddle me. I moan when she rubs up against my cock, which has gone from semi hard to rock hard since the kiss started. My hands cup her ass through the soft material of her dress, while hers pull down on the back of my hair.

A simple kiss turns into something a lot hotter and heavier, just as I hear Clover walk in and say, "Oh look, free porn."

Cara and I still and separate our lips, then turn our heads toward her at the same time. She has her phone out, of course, taking a photo of us.

"Felix won the bet—I shouldn't have underestimated you both. How's that friendship going for you?" She laughs, then disappears down the hallway, the musical sound following her.

Our eyes connect and hold, the tension heavy between us.

I can't think straight when I'm around Cara—all I can see is her. The attraction is so strong and right now, I'd love nothing more than to take her back to my house to have my way with her.

Her phone rings, breaking the trance between us. She clears her throat and answers it.

"Hello?" She pauses as she listens. "Yes, their president, Temper, said for Arrow to call him, but they seem happy to help however they can. Okay. Love you too, Dad." She hangs up and looks to me as she says, "Dad said for me to send him Temper's number and he will touch base with him."

"Okay." I nod, still unable to drag my gaze from her. "I'll send it to you."

She peers down, her dark lashes contrasting against her fair skin. "Do you have to go back to work now?"

I shake my head. "Not right now, no. I have some stuff to do but I can do it later. Why?"

"Let's go back to your house," she decides, an uncertain look appearing on her face. "I mean, if you'd like to."

"Are you kidding me? You read my mind," I say, holding my hand out to her. She takes it and I bring it to my lips, placing a soft kiss there. "After almost losing you, it made me see things more clearly. I don't give a fuck if the timing isn't right. I don't give a fuck about anything, except for you. If you want me, I'm here and I want to be with you. I hope you feel the same way or I'm going to look like a total dumbass right now, but it's the truth."

I know that I'm opening myself up to being vulnerable, and this is the first time I've done that with a woman. Cara could hurt me. She could decide she wants to be alone, or even reconnect with her ex. She could move away. She could, frankly, want nothing to do with me after we fuck a few times.

I don't know how this is going to end, but I want to spend the time with her that I can have. I'd never regret that.

Her answer is to kiss me. "I don't know what the hell we are doing, Decker, but I'm done overthinking it and worrying about it. I want you. Now take me home."

She doesn't have to tell me twice.

We're almost at the front door, hand in hand, when Clover appears behind us and calls out, "Excuse me, you two lovebirds, are you forgetting that people are out to kidnap Cara? You can't just leave without saying anything! Cara, I'm going to kill you."

"There's nowhere safer than with Decker," Cara responds to her best friend. "He's an ex-cop; he knows what he's doing."

I wonder if she knows how those words make me feel. Any man would love to hear his woman say that there's no place safer than with him.

Nothing could make our chests puff out any more.

"I'll have her home in a few hours," I reply. Clover sighs, but agrees. "I won't let anything happen to her."

"Fine, go have dirty sex," Clover calls out as we step outside. "But pay attention! They could already know where Decker lives, or they could have someone following you."

"We know," Cara replies.

Sometimes our baser needs trump all else.

Chapter Twenty-Two

Cara

I know we shouldn't be here, but you know what? That makes it even better.

We don't even make it to the bedroom. As soon as he parks his car in his driveway, it's like an alarm goes off and we're all over each other. He carries me with my legs around him to the front door and even pushes me back against the brick wall near the door, we're kissing and teasing each other before we make it in. If we didn't have people after us, I would have told him to just fuck me right then and there, at the front of the house.

That's how much I want him.

We end up on the kitchen counter, me lying back on the edge, before we finally get to the bedroom.

Decker, now naked and sprawled out on the bed after we've had sex twice, a satisfied expression on his face, makes me happy. And the orgasms he gave me—even happier. I don't have any regrets. In fact, I want him to take me again when I'm able to move.

He's right; with everything that has happened, I don't want to think about the what-ifs. I just want to live my life how I want it, and I want to be unapologetic about it. We might work out, we might not, but either way this is what I want right now.

And I'm taking it.

Future me can worry about the repercussions.

He reaches out to take my hand into his, absently stroking my knuckles. I know I said I wouldn't make the first move again, but I kind of did by telling him that we should come here. When he's affectionate, along with the little speech he gave me back at Clover's, he lets me know that he does feel the same way as me.

I'm feeling good about us.

Which, in turn, makes me feel a little bad about Rhett, who is in danger and has been sent away, while I'm enjoying myself with a new man. I know he's not going to be happy; Dad is right about that. But I can't keep living my life for other people.

Decker, as if he can tell I'm thinking about another man, rolls over and pushes my hair out of my face. "Can I get you anything? Something to eat or drink?"

I shake my head and turn so we are facing each other, up close and looking into each other's eyes. It's quite an intimate moment. How bad is that? We've had sex multiple times, but this moment makes me feel more vulnerable.

"I'm okay, thank you. I think I got what I needed."

His lip twitches. "You and me both. I've been wanting you again so bad, you have no idea. You drive me crazy."

There's something about him that I can't explain, so I know what he's talking about, because I feel the same.

The want. The needs. It's all consuming.

"Then we're even," I whisper huskily.

He kisses me and rolls me on top of him, and then he makes love to me slowly, thoroughly, and without inhibition.

If he wants me to get attached to him, he's doing a good job of it.

I check in with Clover to let her know that we are safe and everything is okay. Decker has an epic security system for his home, so just like Clover's, it's another safe space. Or, at least, as safe as I can get.

We order in Chinese food and eat it naked in bed, talking about everything and anything.

"So you finished a whole degree in marketing and advertising and then realized you didn't want to do it? That sucks."

"Yep," I reply, sighing. "Some people have to learn things the hard way. It seems I am one of those people. Although it feels nice having another degree under my belt as security, if for whatever reason I decide not to teach anymore."

"You mean you can brag about having two degrees?" he teases.

"More like so my parents can," I laugh, putting my takeout container and fork on his side table. "At least you swapped to a similar enough career; mine was completely different."

"A woman of many talents," he compliments, green eyes dancing with amusement.

"I'm sure you've heard this before, but you have the most beautiful eyes I have ever seen," I say, staring into them. "Like seriously, they are fucking turquoise or something. Insane. Sometimes they even look blue. Your eyes are like a mood ring."

"Actually no one has ever told me that before," he replies with a grin, satisfaction coming off him in waves. "But it's now my all-time favorite compliment. And you know what? I can't remember what color eyes I liked the best before you, but it's been brown for a while now."

I shake my head and smile at his charm. "Really? My mud-brown eyes?"

"They aren't mud-brown. They are like chocolate and have a little bit of hazel in them, and they somehow manage to see right through me. So yeah, they are perfect. I fucking love chocolate," he says, keeping his gaze on me. "So now I just have to look at you and show off my ocean eyes whenever you are mad at me? Are they my get-out-of-jail-free cards?"

I roll my eyes. "That compliment went right to your head, didn't it? Now I know why no one else compliments you."

He laughs, and I can't help but just watch him.

He's...something else.

He's perfect, even with all of his flaws, and his cocky attitude and his history for sleeping with God only knows how many women.

He's still perfect to me.

"I don't care about anyone else's compliments, Cara. Just yours alone will get me through the night." He puts the rest of his food aside and cuddles up to me. "I feel...happy."

The way he says it makes it sound like it's a foreign feeling to him. "Lots of sex will do that to you."

But we both know it's not just that.

He's had lots of sex before, but sex with emotion is a whole different ballgame.

"Yeah, with you," he replies quietly, then stands up in all of his naked glory. "I'm going to have a shower—do you want to join me?"

"I'd love to," I reply, checking him out as he disappears into the bathroom.

We are playing a very dangerous game here. I know it, and I know he does.

We just don't care anymore.

And that's what makes it even more terrifying.

"Well, if it isn't Little Miss Hussy," Clover drawls as soon as I step back into her living room.

I smile and sit down across from her. "I know, I shouldn't have gone...but I wanted to and I don't regret it, and I'm in a good mood because I spent all day having hot sex. And I was safe."

"You mean sexually safe, or safe from the people who potentially want to kill you in revenge for what your ex-boyfriend did?"

I pause. "Both."

"Then you better have been having hot sex, because you literally chose Decker's penis over your own life."

I roll my eyes. "You are so dramatic." Fire comes over to cuddle me. "Hello, my gorgeous girl."

"Don't kiss her, we know where your mouth has been," Clover mutters under her breath, unable to keep a straight face. "Are you going to tell me all about it or not?"

"Are you going to keep giving me shit or not?" I reply, arching my brow.

"I'm sorry, but I want you to be safe. I was having high anxiety thinking about you getting railed and not paying attention and someone taking advantage of that and shooting you or something."

"You were thinking about me getting railed?" I ask, covering Fire's ears.

Clover laughs and shrugs. "You know what I mean. So no regrets, huh?"

"None."

"It's been a while since I've seen you like this," she confesses quietly. She shrugs, tucking her dark hair back behind her ear. "Like you're living again. Like you're happy. Present. Living your best life. Look at you; you can't stop smiling."

"I feel happy," I agree, ducking my face. "Maybe it's selfish, I don't know, but I like him."

My phone chimes with a text from Con, who I've been in contact with pretty much every day since I saw her.

Con: When are you free this week? Want to go out for dinner and a movie or something?

"How do I explain to Con that I can't go out to play right now because people are trying to kidnap me as revenge for something my biker ex-boyfriend did?" I ask out loud. I don't want Con to feel like I'm blowing her off. I do want to get to know her, but the timing is just really bad.

Clover winces, her eyes on her daughter, who is now sitting on the floor playing with her toys. "Yeah, I don't know about that one. I mean, you don't want her dragged into this bullshit, too. I don't think she would be able to fight off two grown men like you did."

Clover is right. I don't want Con to be tied into any of this, and I don't want to see her get hurt. It's safer for her if she's not seen with me in public at all.

Cara: Hey, things are a little hectic here right now. Do you mind if we make it next week or so?

Con: No problem. Hope things are okay?"

Cara: I'm fine, just haven't been feeling that great.

I mean, technically not a lie.

Con: I hope you feel better.

Yeah, me too.

Chapter Twenty-Three

Decker

After dropping Cara back home, I head into my office to finish up some of the last cases I'll be working on until all of this drama is over.

Nadia comes in and I get up to give her a big hug. "I owe you one."

"For what?" she asks, looking up at me suspiciously.

"What do you mean for what? You talked the MC into helping Cara. You are literally the best friend a guy could ask for."

She pauses. "Did you ever think they're doing it for you? You've helped them out in the past, and they consider you a friend. Why wouldn't they help you? Trust me, I didn't even have to beg them. I just mentioned it, and they took it from there."

"Really?"

She nods and steps around me to head to her desk. "Nice that you think I have that much pull, though."

"Well, Trade does, and he'd do anything for you, so…"

"That is true, but this time I didn't have to do any

convincing. You helped me in finding their bad apple and getting Ariel's murderer, so as they see it, they owe you multiple favors," she says, opening up her laptop.

That was the case that really opened my eyes to how frustrated I was at being a cop. Nadia and I knew the man convicted of Ariel's murder was innocent, but no one would listen because he had been convicted of other crimes before. But we found the guy who had really done it, and he had been sitting under everyone's noses.

"What are you doing here anyway? I thought you were taking some time off to look after Cara," she says, looking at me over the screen.

"I wanted to tie up some loose ends. I still have one case that I haven't wrapped up."

"Send me the information, I'll handle it," she offers, shrugging. "No big deal. And we won't take any new cases until we both have the time to invest in them."

"Is this the perk of having two incomes?" I tease.

She pauses and then laughs. "Why yes, yes it is. And because I now own the space, I don't have to worry about being kicked out if I don't pay rent."

I sit down and send her the case details. "Thank you for doing this for me."

"Any time," she replies with a smile. "You'd do it for me, and besides, who am I to stand in the way of true love?"

"And to think you were doing so well at not being annoying," I grumble.

"Not ready to hear the L word?" she presses, amusement dancing in her brown eyes. "Am I making you feel uncomfortable, Decker? I'll never understand men. They are too scared to say they are in love with someone, but would take a bullet for that same person without thinking."

"Maybe dying is a better alternative," I joke. "She wants to meet you, by the way."

"Well, I'd say drop in whenever you want, but you have people after you, so maybe don't," she says as she stands up. "However, we can meet you at the clubhouse or something, if that works?"

"Fair, and that sounds good."

"I'll sort out this case—you get out of here," she says. "Oh, and give Atlas a call. He's at Fast & Fury waiting on his instructions for him, Aries and Diesel."

"I will do. Thank you."

"Any time."

I leave the office and head home. When I sit on my bed, it still smells like Cara's perfume. It distracts me as I send Felix a text, asking him where is he is.

Felix: Just leaving the station. You at home? I'll drop in.

Me: Yep.

I've finished tidying my room and changing my bedsheets when he arrives, knocking loudly.

"Hey," he greets when I open the door. He's still in his detective uniform, and a little bit of me misses that uniform. "Cara with Clover?"

I nod. "Where do we want the MC members? I have to give them a call and tell them what the plan is."

We sit down and come up with a plan, to have one of us and one of the Knights watching Cara at all times. Felix connects his home security to my phone too, so I know what's happening there and can be on call to help if something goes down.

"What do you think they will do next?" I ask.

He leans back and stretches his arms out over the back of the couch. "If they know the Knights are also now involved, they would be stupid to keep targeting her, but I don't know. They are bold. I think it's only a matter of time. I know Clover can handle herself, but it's scary knowing Sapphire is also there and something could go down."

"That's why we leave one of the Knights there keeping watch at all times. We won't let anything happen to your girls, any of them," I promise. "And if it gets worse, we get Fire out of there and to somewhere safe."

He nods in agreement. "Yeah, we have a few safe spots we can leave her. I'm hoping it doesn't come to that."

"We've got this, brother. We've been through worse."

His lip twitches. "I know. It's just a whole different fucking ballgame when people you love are involved and could get hurt."

"Not happening, Felix."

"I hear Cara spent the morning here with you," he says with a smirk, crossing his arms over his chest. "You want to talk about that?"

"No, I sure as hell do not," I reply, mirroring his body language. "And I couldn't even if I wanted to, because I have no idea. My plan right now is to keep her alive. I can worry about all the rest later."

"I'm just saying—I've never seen you like this with a woman before. Any woman."

"I know."

He nods. "She's a good woman, and I think the two of you make a beautiful couple."

"Getting ahead of yourself—"

"Welcome to the Wind Dragons madhouse, Decker. Happy to have some company here." He laughs, standing up and heading for the door. "You call the Knights, I'm going to go home and watch over the girls."

He closes the door behind him and I'm left pondering his words. I send Simone a text.

Me: There's some shit going down. Be careful. Don't trust anyone. Call me if you need me. Better yet, why don't you come and stay here?

Simone: What's going on? I'm fine. I have Whitney. I'll be careful.

Me: Make sure your cameras are on and everything is locked.

Simone: Always.

She's so stubborn. The world could be coming to an end and she'd still tell me that she's fine. But you know what? I believe it. Simone is one of the strongest women I've ever known. She fits in well with Cara and Clover. She might not be a badass martial artist, but she's smart and emotionally unbreakable. And she's right, Whitney *is* a good guard dog.

I send Cara a text to check in with her.

Me: You all good?

She replies instantly.

Cara: Yeah, I'm fine.

Me: Okay, good, just checking.

Cara: Something goes down you will know it.

I miss her. I want to tell her that, but I don't.

Me: I'll be over soon.

Cara: Okay. Bring some food.

I laugh at her message and reply, asking her what she wants. Damn, I'll drive all over the city to get her exactly what she wants if I have to.

It's in this moment I know that I am truly in trouble.

I finish cleaning up, call up Atlas and tell him the plan, and for them to make a roster to take turns. I grab my gun and then drive off to buy food for Cara, Clover, Felix, Sapphire and myself. I know what would have happened if I showed up without food for Clover too, and I'm not that stupid.

When I show up with the burgers Cara requested, her smile is so worth it.

"Thank you." She beams, taking one of the bags from me. "I'm starving."

Clover appears like she smelled the food and sighs happily when I hand her the other bag. "You get my tick of approval for this act alone."

We sit down at the table and eat. Felix comes out of the shower and joins us. "You spoke to the Knights?"

I nod. "Atlas will be here tonight for the night watch, and then they will take turns. So we have backup, and from now on someone will go with Cara whenever she leaves the house, and someone will always be back here to make sure Clover and Fire are safe, too."

I watch Cara eating and enjoying every single bite, doing a little happy dance, and I make note to always bring her food whenever she wants it, because she's never looked happier and more in her element.

She has just swallowed her last bite when we hear gunshots go off, glass shattering.

"Get under the table!" I call to everyone, while I grab my gun and run to the front with Felix at my side.

A car speeds off, tires screeching behind them. We step outside and take in the damage. Multiple bullets have completely shattered the glass window, and tire tracks are left on the lawn. The men had run up to the gate and shot from between the gaps. They couldn't make it in here, but they obviously found a loophole, literally.

"Let's see if we can get their license plate number from the security footage," Felix suggests, jaw going tight. "Those bastards are lucky no one got hurt."

"They are telling us that they know where she is," I reply, looking him in the eye. "It's a warning. I think we need to stop sitting around and waiting for them to make the moves. We need to take this into our own hands."

Felix might still have a badge, but I don't.

And I'll do whatever I need to do to protect Cara.

Chapter Twenty-Four

Cara

I'm still holding on to Clover and Fire when Atlas walks in. "Looks like I missed all the fun."

The fact that this gang shot into this house where my goddaughter lives absolutely terrifies me. This house has every safety measure, and she still could have gotten hurt. We all could have.

"I need to leave, I can't put you all in danger," I say to Clover, wanting to cry. If anything happened to any of them, I don't know what I would do. I'd rather die myself than lose one of them.

"No, you don't. They know where we live now—we are already a target," she comments, looking down at her daughter. Fire has been handling all the commotion like a boss, without any fuss or tears. "I can drop Fire off somewhere safe. I think it's best that she does go, after what just happened. And that way I can be out the front with the guns instead of hiding under the table." She turns to me. "They fucked with the wrong people, Cara. No one is going to try to hurt my family. It's about time I came out of motherfucking leave."

"Clo—"

She kisses my cheek and then goes to speak with Felix, and I know she's telling him her plan. Fire will be sent away somewhere safe until this is all over with, and Clover gets to be in the action without worrying about her daughter getting hurt.

I hate that all of this is because of me.

Because of Rhett.

Because of the MC.

Decker sits next to me and pulls me into his arms. I close my eyes tight, and after holding myself together all of this time, I finally let myself fall apart.

"Someone could have died because of me," I cry into his black T-shirt. "Can you get me out of here? I don't want them to get hurt because of me. There was a baby in here!"

He rubs my back, and I hate that he is seeing me this weak. "We can stay at my house, if you want to. I'll let everyone know."

"I do." I nod, realizing that no matter what Clo says, I need to separate myself from them. It also means I'm putting Decker at risk, but being with him feels safe.

I'm not scared of dying. But losing someone I love? That is what terrifies me. I think there is only one thing that could break me, make me lose my mind in grief, and that would be it.

Anything else I could survive.

"Sapphire is going to go somewhere else so she will be safe, and we are going to fix this, all right?" he promises me, his deep, soothing voice calming me down. "No one got hurt. And they are going to regret this, you hear me?"

I nod, but stay silent.

How are we going to take down an entire gang? A child of theirs was hurt, and maybe they want revenge, an eye for an eye.

And we have only one child in our family.

"It's safer if Sapphire goes," I say out loud, reassuring myself. "She needs to be protected at all costs."

"She will be."

I sit up and wipe my tears away. "But I want to go to your house. I'm going to pack my stuff."

I don't want to put them in danger again.

And Clover is right about one thing—we should be out there guns blazing, not hiding under fucking tables. I might not be a cop or a member of the FBI like she was, but I'm not untrained. This is my world too, and I've survived it so far.

I touch the stubble on Decker's cheek.

I'm not leaving this world now, not when I only just started truly living.

Pressing a kiss against his lips, I say, "Tell me what the plan is. I'm helping. I'm not sitting here and letting others fight my fight. I'm there, with you all, every step of the way."

"Cara—"

"I don't need protecting, Decker. What I need is my freedom back, and the safety of the people I love."

He kisses me back, and opens his green eyes as he pulls away. "Okay."

"Okay?" I ask, brows lifting in surprise. "You're not going to give me any shit?"

He laughs. "I know how strong and badass you are,

Cara. And I'll be there to have your back. No matter what."

I push him back against the black leather and kiss him more deeply this time, until I hear someone's throat clearing. I glance up to see Atlas standing there. "You sure you need protecting? You look fine to me."

I move off Decker and sit up straight. "Atlas, right?"

He nods and takes a seat opposite us, crossing his legs at the ankles. "The car was most likely stolen, no plates, so there's no lead there. But here's a fun fact: I actually know someone in the gang."

"Who?" Decker asks.

Atlas rubs the back of his neck, his blue eyes uncertain. "Yeah, see, this is where shit is going to get messy. It's my stepbrother, CJ. No, we aren't close, but I figure I could try to find some shit out from him."

Decker and I share a look. "Your stepbrother? So their reach is bigger than we thought. They aren't going to move here, they already *are* here."

Atlas nods slowly. He's a handsome man, his blond hair short on the sides and longer on top. "Yeah, and I told Temper the second I heard. They call themselves the FC, or the Forgotten Children. Temper thinks it's good—we could have an in."

The Forgotten Children.

It's nice to put a name to the madness.

"Are you okay with that?" I ask him boldly.

He winces. "Yeah, look. I have no love for the FC, but I wouldn't want anything to happen to my stepbrother. We might not be close but…it's complicated."

"Family, right," I reply with a small smile.

"Exactly." He looks to Decker. "She's a beautiful

woman, you know that? I can see why you are willing to protect her with everything that you have."

He heads outside, leaving Decker and me alone with those last words.

"He's right," he says, reaching for my hand. "On both accounts."

I smile and duck my head. There's so much going on right now, but his words are always comforting. He's been my rock through this whole thing, and I don't know what I would do without him.

"Well, lucky for me that my long-lost half sister contacted you to track me down then, isn't it?" I reply, and lick my suddenly dry lips.

I want to tell him how I'm feeling, but I don't know if now is the right time, and things are just so new. However, being in this situation has shown his true colors, and I can't ignore that.

He's loyal.

He's brave.

He's sweet.

And he's damn good in bed.

There's no point ignoring the fact that he's standing by me through a kidnapping and now a shooting, and yeah, he's not going anywhere. He's here knowing that people are trying to kill us.

I don't know how I got so lucky, but the thing about me? I go after what I want.

And I want Seth Decker.

Chapter Twenty-Five

Decker

Felix organizes some men to come in and fix the windows, while Clover spends her time researching bulletproof glass, calling them an investment that she needs in her life.

Faye and Sin return to pick up baby Fire and take her somewhere safe. Even with Cara coming to stay at my place, Clover decided it was still safer for Fire somewhere else.

Clover clings to her daughter, kissing her head over and over again. "Mama is going to miss you."

I know Cara feels terrible that this has to happen, so I make sure to stand next to her and offer her my support. I've never been really good at comforting people—I'm more of a suffer-in-silence kind of guy—but with her I want to at least try.

I watch as she says goodbye to her goddaughter, and note the sadness in those beautiful brown eyes. As soon as Fire leaves her arms, Cara turns and hugs me, burying her face in my chest. I hold her tightly. Glancing over her, I notice Faye and Sin observing me closely.

"Look after her," Faye says, and I nod.

Clover cries after they leave, and Felix takes her to their room. I sit out in the living area with Cara, watching the new windows being installed. Atlas watches from the outside, checking the perimeter. I appreciate him being here, because it allows me to relax a little bit more.

"It won't be for too long; she will be back," I whisper to Cara, stroking her hair. She has her head in my lap, her feet up on the couch, her green socks poking out. "And she will be safe."

"I know," she replies, sighing deeply. "I know it's what's best for her, but do you know how hard it was to see my best friend crying because her kid had to go? Clover hardly ever cries. And to know this is all because of my bullshit—"

"It's to do with MC bullshit, which is all of your bullshit," I remind her. "Clover included. No one would blame this on you, Cara. Like you said, this is how you grew up, this is a part of the lifestyle that you are all in, not just you. Clover was sad to say bye to her child, like any mother would be, but she knows it is the right thing to do right now. This isn't on just you. It's an issue that touches everyone. You just happened to be dating the wrong guy at the wrong time and now you are a main target."

She makes a sound of disgruntlement. "And I haven't even spoken to Rhett. I know they haven't told him about what's happening over here."

"How do you know that?"

"Because then he would be here," she says, shrugging. "He's not a coward. He wouldn't be able to hide if he knew they tried to kidnap me, or that they shot up Clover's house. He would be here."

I know that she didn't say anything that's not true, but the way that she speaks about him makes me feel… I don't know. Jealous? Whatever it is, I don't fucking like it. Not that I'd ever let her know that. Like I said before, suffer in silence.

"Okay, well, I guess that's why no one is telling him," I reply, and clear my throat a little. "And maybe that's what the FC want. For him to come out and face what has happened, and that's why they are going after you."

"Yeah, I'm the bait," she replies, sounding like she has accepted her fate. "I just don't know how we are going to solve this. We can't fight a whole gang, I mean, the MC could, but we'd all end up in prison, and no one wants that. We can't kill them. They aren't going to go anywhere either—people hold grudges for a long time. I don't want my future kids to have to watch out for the FC because of what is going on right now."

I wince at the picture she is painting. "Yeah, that doesn't sound like much fun, does it?"

"Nope. They aren't going to forgive a kid being hurt, though—this shit runs deep. They'd be angry and they want their pound of flesh as revenge."

It should be Rhett giving them that pound of flesh, not Cara.

"We will find a way that ends the feud but keeps us all out of prison," I promise her. "We can ask Atlas's stepbrother what they would need to end this shit. Otherwise, the Wind Dragons are going to have to step up and handle it from their end. There's only so much we can do."

"I know. We just need to stay alive," she grumbles, looking up at me. "Thank you for being here. I know that you don't have to, and it means a lot to me. You are…one of a kind, you know that?"

I'm smiling as I lean down and kiss her. "I'm crazy about you, Cara. Can't be letting anything happen to you when I've finally found someone that I like."

Her eyes soften, but I don't miss the amusement there either. "Trust me, the feeling is mutual. And it's nice to hear you say it. Especially when I'm lying here, feeling sorry for myself, and not exactly in my finest form."

I laugh just as Clover comes out and sits next to us. "We will be okay," she tells her best friend.

"I'm sorry," Cara whispers.

"It's not your fault," Clover replies, tone hardening. "And don't you ever think that. I'm sad to see my baby go, but it's for her own good."

"Clo, I'm going to Decker's place."

"But—"

Cara holds up her hand. "I love you, but I will not bring this on you."

Felix agrees with the plan, liking the idea of moving Cara around and therefore not being an easy target. Cara packs some things to move in with me for a few days.

"What do we do now?" Clover asks, shifting on her feet, looking like she's actually excited for some action to happen.

"I'm going to get Cara settled at my house, and I think we need to speak to Atlas about talking to his stepbrother." I don't want to put the guy in a bad position, but it's all we have right now, and having some inside information would be fucking great.

"You know him the best," Clover prompts.

"I'll come with you," Cara suggests, and the two of us head out front, where Atlas is sitting on the mailbox and having a smoke.

He arches his brow when he sees us. "Let me guess, you want me to talk to CJ?"

"Only if you don't mind," Cara says, tucking her hair back behind her ear. "We don't want to put you in an awkward position or anything, so you can say no. We just don't know how we are going to solve all of this without some bloodshed, so if your stepbrother could help us in any way, that would be great. I don't want anyone to get hurt, and please tell him we are so sorry for what happened to that boy. We would never want any children to ever be harmed in any sort of way, no matter what was going on."

Atlas studies Cara, and then nods. "Okay, I'll speak to him after I'm done here, when Aries comes to swap with me."

"Thank you, Atlas. We owe you one," she says, reaching out and touching his arm.

I grit my teeth until she removes her hand.

Atlas brings his eyes to me. "Yes, you do."

Great, looks like that's a marker I'm going to be repaying.

But fuck it, I'll worry about that when the time comes.

Because she is worth it.

Chapter Twenty-Six

Cara

"I thought you had to go home," I say to Atlas after he knocks at the door. I'm standing there with my bag about to leave, and he's dressed differently, in a gray T-shirt instead of black, so he must have gone home and gotten changed.

Decker laughs from next to me. "That's not Atlas— that's Aries, his twin brother. Come on in, Aries."

He steps in, and it's then that I notice a few slight differences between the two. Aries's hair is a little lighter, and his eyes are green instead of blue. But aside from that, the two of them look exactly the same. "No one told me Atlas had a twin."

Aries just looks at me but stays silent, and I share a look with Decker, who simply smirks. "He's a lot quieter than his brother."

"I see."

Decker shows Aries around and gives him a quick briefing while I make some dinner for us all. It feels weird to still do everyday tasks with everything going on, but everyone still has to eat.

When my phone rings with a private number, I answer it warily. "Hello?"

"Cara, it's me," Rhett says. "I'm sorry I haven't called. I tried before I left."

"Are you okay?" I ask, clasping the phone.

"I'm fine. Arrow sent me away and told me to keep a low profile. I just got a burner phone so I could call you. Are you okay?" he asks.

I hesitate before answering. "I heard about what happened."

He goes silent. "I fucked up. I didn't want anyone to get hurt. Especially a kid."

The truth is, all is not fair in love and war. There are some things that will never be wins, and civilians, women or children being hurt are one of those things. These are the things that would haunt you every day, the things you can't escape from when you close your eyes at night.

"I know."

"I just wanted to make sure you were okay."

"I'm at Clover's."

"Okay, good. I'll see you when I get back then. Whenever that may be," he says, and there's a shuffling noise in the background. "Tell Clo I love her. I love you both."

"Will do."

I want to tell him that I love him too, because I do. I'm just not in love with him anymore. I'll always love him. But I don't want to give him the wrong idea either, so I just stay silent.

We end the call, and I sit down at the dining table and wonder if I did the right thing by not telling him the truth—that shit has gone to hell—but then he would come right here and probably end up dead. If the MC wanted him to know, they would have told him themselves, so I suppose I need to go along with that. I just don't like lying to him, and I know he's going to be angry when he finds out the truth.

I hear Clover talking to Aries and calling him Atlas too, and laugh to myself that it wasn't just me making that assumption.

After we finish eating, Decker and I get in the car and drive to his house. When we get there, he checks the perimeter while I settle into his bedroom. It's quieter here, and it's nice to have a moment to myself. My phone beeps with a message.

Clover: I miss you already, come home.

I smile at her text.

Decker and I spend the rest of the day at home, being lazy, and we even have dinner in bed, talking, planning and organizing for all kinds of different scenarios. I find Decker watching the live security feed on his phone before I take a shower and then hop on the soft white bedsheets to cuddle up next to him. "What a clusterfuck of a day."

"We're all okay, that's all that matters," he murmurs, putting his phone away and giving me all of his attention. He rests his chin on the top of my head. "I'm sure we can find a way to make this day better."

I grin as he rolls on top, making sure not to put his weight on me, and presses his lips against mine. My fingers run through his hair, his masculine scent driving me crazy. I'm so glad that I'm here with him, and it's a little terrifying how much I enjoy having him around. It's like we've known each other for a long time. I don't know how else to explain it. We just get each other. And it's more than just the amazing sex, it's something else, something I can't name.

He's about to start undressing me, his lips on my neck, when we hear a knock on the front door. Decker grabs his phone to check the security feed, and sees that it's Aries and Atlas both standing there. Atlas has a bloody nose from the looks of it, and he's holding a tissue over it.

"Stay here," he says, rushing out of the room.

I quickly send Clo a text letting her know something must be up, and follow him instead, hoping they aren't here with any bad news. I watch while Decker opens the door. When Atlas steps inside in the light, I can see that he indeed has been hit in the nose—the tissue in his hand is covered in blood.

"What happened to you?" I ask, frowning. "Are you okay?"

"I'm fine," he replies. "Sorry to come over so late, but I just spoke to CJ."

He just came from speaking to his stepbrother and he has blood on his face?

"He hit you?" I ask.

Atlas stretches his neck from side to side. "Let's just say the last time I saw him we didn't end on good terms."

Aries silently heads back outside, to keep watch, I'm assuming, and then we are interrupted by Clo and Felix's arrival, and Clo is dressed in her all-black fighting gear. She kind of looks like a ninja. I bet she has at least three weapons on her. We all sit down to hear what Atlas has to say.

"So he didn't tell you shit, then?" Decker guesses.

"Nope, he did. Like I said, family is complicated."

"What did you find out?" Clover asks.

"The kid who got shot, he's going to be okay. The bullet hit him in the leg, but he's their leader Marko's son. And Marko doesn't want to let it go. He's pissed and not thinking straight, and he wants revenge," Atlas explains, bringing his gaze to me. "They want Rhett, but they can't find him and they know where you are. They think you are his woman, and I told CJ otherwise. He said he will try to tell Marko that, but he doesn't think he will care, because Rhett would still care about you, current girlfriend or not."

"So he's not willing to settle this at all?" Decker asks, eyes narrowing. "He's just happy to let this war keep going until people are dead?"

"Like I said, he's not thinking straight. CJ said he will try to talk to him, but I think the men have been trying to this whole time. End of the day, they will follow their leader's orders. You all know how it goes," Atlas says with a shrug.

"How much sway does CJ hold?" Decker asks him, jaw tense. "Do you think he could make Marko see some sense?"

"I don't know," Atlas replies, looking out across the street. "I guess we will have to wait and see, and stay alert until then. CJ said he will call me if he has any updates."

"Thank you, Atlas," I say. "Sorry you had to go there and get hit."

Atlas touches his nose and smirks. "I deserved it. Last time we saw each other, I slept with his girlfriend."

"Well, that would do it," Clover mutters, eyes going wide.

Decker wraps his arm around me, pulling me close to him absently, as if I could suddenly be next.

Awkward.

Atlas heads home, and Decker offers Felix and Clo his spare bedroom. We have a chat about what Atlas just told us, but after we go to our separate rooms, Decker and I soon start carrying on from where we left off, with me making the first move by jumping into his arms and kissing him. We can't seem to keep our hands off each other, even in the middle of a crisis, or maybe it's because we need a distraction right now.

Decker slowly undresses me, teasing me, his lips covering every inch of my skin. He starts to go down on me and I moan loudly, then still, realizing that Clover and Felix can most likely hear us. The house is dead silent and there's nothing to muffle the sound.

I'm extremely close with Clo, but we are not *that* close.

"Wait a minute," I say. He instantly lets go and sits up, watching me.

"Is everything okay?" he asks, listening for any noise around us.

"No. I mean, yes, it's fine. I'm just really loud when you do that thing with your tongue. And I don't want Clover to hear me having sex! That would be traumatizing. She's like my sister," I whisper-yell at him.

Decker seems to find this amusing, his eyes sparkling with humor. "We don't have to if you don't want to, Cara. We can just cuddle."

His raging erection is still evident. I appreciate that he doesn't mind putting my mind at ease even though I'm the one who started this whole thing by practically jumping him when we got back to the room.

"I can hear everything that you are saying!" Clover suddenly calls out from her room, making me freeze.

Oh my God.

Why me?

Decker laughs out loud, the asshole, and I'm pretty sure I can hear Clover and Felix laughing from the spare bedroom, also.

"And you're right; I don't want to hear it. I'm going to put the TV on really loudly so it doesn't get awkward," she yells.

Stupid paper-thin walls.

"Thank you," Decker calls back to her, and then I hear her laughter, louder this time.

Don't get me wrong, I know she has sex, and a lot of it, but that doesn't mean I want to hear her and vice versa. I can hear the TV loud as ever now, the *Supernatural* theme song, which makes me feel a whole lot better.

I smile at Decker, and he smiles back even wider.

Clover really is the best friend ever.

Chapter Twenty-Seven

Decker

I give Simone a call to check in on her and to see if she needs anything. She assures me she's fine and she's been careful, which is a relief to me. She also demands answers as to what's going on, so I give her a brief rundown. She's obviously concerned, but seems more worried about me than herself. I promise her it will all be okay.

Diesel comes to my house to take over for Aries, and I don't miss the way he subtly sneaks a second glance at Cara.

Yeah, no chance.

Cara disappears and comes out of the bedroom twenty minutes later, freshly showered and dressed in taupe track pants and a matching hoodie, one that shows some of her stomach.

"You look cute," I say, my eyes devouring her greedily.

"Have a good night?" Clover asks, smirking from my coffee machine.

Cara's eyes narrow ever so slightly. "I did. Did you?"

"Always," Clover responds, turning around and

handing me and Cara some coffee. "I can't remember the last time I had a full night's sleep. It would have been when I was pregnant. What a luxury. It's crazy the things I took for granted before becoming a mom."

"Don't get used to it," Cara teases, pulling out a stool at the breakfast table and sitting down. "What's on the agenda today? I don't like feeling like we're trapped here, just sitting targets."

"I know what you mean," I agree. "Why don't we do something fun? With us all together, it's not like anyone is left alone and vulnerable."

Cara's eyes light up. "What do you have in mind?"

I think it over. "It's a nice day today. What if we went to a lake or something and had a swim? Somewhere with no one else around."

Cara's smile widens and she does a little happy dance, the same one she does when she eats sometimes. "I think that sounds perfect. Clover?"

"Hell yeah, count us in. I can pick us up some lunch on the way," Clover replies, tapping her finger on her cheek. "And wine. And if we die, at least we die happy."

Felix appears at that moment and scowls at his wife's casual talk of our demise. "No one is dying."

I pull out my phone and search for a spot, not too far away in case something happens here, but far enough that it won't be too busy. "Okay, I think I've found a spot. We have to do a little walking to get there, though…"

I show them the photos of the swimming spot, and everyone is instantly onboard. It has a beautiful waterfall and crystal-clear water. "There will probably be some people there, but hopefully not too many considering it's not that easy to get to."

"We're going to a lake?" Felix asks, perking up. "Now we're talking."

We all go and get ready, and I'm not going to lie—I'm excited to see Cara in a bikini. She doesn't disappoint, coming out of the room in a red bikini, one that shows just a little hint of underboob. She looks amazing.

And the sexiest thing about her is that she is confident about herself. That is the biggest turn-on of all.

"Holy shit," I mutter, asking her to turn around.

She laughs and does a little turn. My eyes are glued to her perfect ass.

I make a little growling sound and prowl up to her, just as Felix calls out, "We're all bringing our guns, right?"

If that isn't a slap back into reality, I don't know what is.

We walk along the pebbles, and I remain right behind Cara, enjoying the view indeed. She put a little wrap around her bikini, her hair tied up in a messy bun. She looks beautiful.

"I can't wait to jump into that water," Clover says, eying the clear water.

"Thank you for making us come here today. I think we all needed it," Cara says.

Cara needed it more than anyone.

"No need to thank me," I say, bringing her hand to my lips and kissing her knuckles.

She smiles widely, and we all head down toward the

water. When we get there, we all strip down and jump in. Cara floats on her back, staring up at the blue sky.

"Looks like we got the spot to ourselves after all," I muse, looking around.

"I know, how lucky are we?" she replies.

We spend the next few hours in the water and having a picnic that Clover set up for lunch. When it's time for us to head back, I feel a little sad, because I know that our carefree time is now over, and reality will soon kick back in.

Proof of this is when we get back to the car. My phone reception kicks in and I instantly get a call from Atlas.

"Where are you guys?" he asks.

"About an hour away from home. Is everything okay?"

He goes silent for a few long seconds. "We have a small problem."

"I'll be there soon." I look around to Cara, Clover and Felix. "Atlas said that we have a small problem."

Felix checks the security at his home, eyes going wide and a loud curse falling from his lips. "Yeah, we fucking do have a problem."

"What?"

He shows me the footage. Looks like while we were gone a few members of the FC went to their house. Except this time, Atlas caught one of them.

"So there's a hostage waiting for us at home with a gun to his head," I mutter, turning to Cara, who looks understandably concerned.

"What are we going to do with him?" she asks, brow furrowing.

"I don't know. Let's just get home as quickly as we can."

We buckle up, and I step on the gas.

Nothing like having a hostage at the house held by gunpoint by your biker friend to make you want to drive home fast.

"Maybe we could use him to make a deal?" Cara suggests, looking out the window in thought. "We have to use this situation to our advantage somehow."

"Yes. We can obviously try to get information out of him, but maybe we can blackmail him or something. Find something on them all. I don't know what yet, but I'm going to play this to our advantage," Clover adds.

"I'm glad you're both on our side," I say to her and Cara. "I just love how three of them showed up and Atlas, by himself, scared two off and managed to capture the other."

He obviously is pretty skilled, and whether he learned that on the streets or somewhere else, I'm thankful for it. The Knights of Fury MC have some strong men to have at your back, and I'm glad I reached out to them.

"Do we get the cops and FBI involved, or is that going to bite us in the ass somehow?" Clover asks, sighing. "Something might have to happen that we want to hide under the rug."

Felix winces. This is why I left the force. I can't imagine what Felix goes through being married to Clover and having in-laws who are part of an MC.

"I don't know. What did they think they could do, just walk in and take her?" Felix asks, shaking his head. "Do you think they even plan things out or just decide in that moment?"

"I have no idea, but hopefully we can find out some new insight," Clover says as she pats her husband's shoulder. "I think you should sit this one out. We don't want to get you into any trouble."

"I think both of you should sit this one out," I say to them. "We got this. You don't need to cross any lines."

I can do it for them.

They share a look, and I know they are both wondering how to best approach this.

Welcome to the gray zone.

By the time we get to Felix's home, the sun is about to set and we park in the garage. We get out, our guns ready just in case some shit has gone down since we last checked in with Atlas.

We find Atlas sitting on the couch, watching TV— *Married at First Sight*, to be more precise—while the other man has been tied up and gagged, sitting opposite him.

"About time you got here," he says, turning the TV off and facing us. "I got you all a little present."

We look at the dark-haired, dark-eyed man, and I have to wonder just how this is about to play out.

"Run us through what happened exactly," I say, sharing a glance with Felix.

"I did a drive around to check the perimeter, and I saw this guy and two of his friends circle the neighborhood, once, and then twice. So I followed them. Eventually they parked a few houses down and walked over. They had guns, but I caught this guy from behind and threatened to kill him unless they put their weapons down. They backed down and complied, and then I aimed my gun at them and told them unless they left I would kill them both right here and now.

"They ran. This one, unfortunately for him, was stuck with me for questioning. I knocked him out and brought him inside."

We all stare at the man in question, who looks both angry and scared.

I look at Cara, but before I can open my mouth, she reads my mind.

"No, I'm staying for this." She looks to Clover. "We all are."

Okay then.

I'm about to interrogate a witness, all with Cara watching over my shoulder.

Guess it's time for her to see the other side of me.

Chapter Twenty-Eight

Cara

Decker finds the hostage's wallet in his pockets with his ID.

His name is Ryder West. We let the man speak.

"We were just told to come to this house, and if we saw her"—he nods at me—"to bring her in. Marko also said if we want to have some fun, we could."

"What type of 'fun' was he referring to?" Decker asks, as he rolls his sleeves up and braces himself over Ryder. I know it's inappropriate, but Decker is seriously fucking hot right now. The veins in his arm are pulsing and his stance is all in control and alpha.

He is in his element, going back to what he would do when he was a cop.

Ryder's lips tighten. "When we saw no one was home, I parked the car down the road and figured we'd fuck up the house. Have some fun."

"And you're okay with that?" Felix asks, pushing off the couch and standing next to Decker. I notice Clover watching his every move, and I know she's feeling the exact way I am right now.

Ryder smirks. "You're all bikers—like you can judge anything we do. We listen to Marko. He's our leader, and if he says we can have some fun, we're going to do just that."

"Actually we're not all bikers, he's a cop," Decker says, looking at Felix. "You came to a cop's house and tried this bullshit. Not very smart, don't you think? We could kill you right now and cover it up if we wanted to."

I know Decker is bluffing. Despite all of his talk about leaving the police force, he still has a strong code of ethics. Besides, Felix would never do something like that. Following the letter of the law is in his blood.

The color drains from Ryder's face. "We were told you were all a part of the Wind Dragons MC. There was no mention of a cop."

Felix pulls out his badge and shows him it. Ryder looks like he's going to be sick.

"Looks like your boss sent you here not giving a fuck if you end up in prison," Clover comments, shrugging. "And you compare yourself to bikers? Bikers wouldn't do that. We look after each other."

"Tell us what they want to do with Cara," Decker asks, and I know this is why he didn't really want me to be here. I'm going to hear firsthand what's going to happen to me if they catch me.

Ryder looks me dead in the eyes as he replies, "I don't know. He said she is to be untouched and brought to him. His kid got hurt—don't you think that's an eye for an eye?"

"That was an accident, and he's okay now," I say. "So why hold on to this grudge and drag out a war? Someone is going to get killed. And I didn't do anything at all, so you are targeting innocent people now. Maybe you all belong in prison."

"I could make that happen," Felix adds.

"What are you going to do with me?" Ryder asks, looking up at Decker. "If anything happens to me, Marko is just going to get angrier and that's not going to help. You can't win."

"He's right," Atlas replies, eying Decker. "I know you want to beat the shit out of him right now, but it's not going to help. I think you should just get him arrested. Let him know the law is involved."

Felix whispers something to Clover and excuses himself to go outside.

Ryder laughs, but I can tell it's a bluff. "Do you know how many FC are in prison? I'd be welcomed there like a king."

Decker, apparently unable to take it anymore, clocks Ryder right in the face.

"We could send him in there with a rumor that he's a rat," Clover, the evil mastermind, suggests. "Then they'd just kill him instead of welcoming him."

Ryder freezes and spits out the blood from his mouth. "You couldn't do that."

"We have people everywhere too," she replies, smirking. "Try me."

He considers his options. "What do you want from me?"

"We want some information about the FC," Decker states, getting straight to business.

"Then I *will* be a rat!"

"Yeah, but no one else will know that," Clover says,

standing up in front of him. "You came to a cop's house. You guys have shot up said cop's house. Did you think there wasn't going to be any repercussions for that? Oh, by the way, should I add that I'm also a member of the FBI? You're fucked, Ryder. So work with us, or against us. Which one is it going to be?"

He swallows, hard. "Marko will kill me."

"So will we," Decker says in a deep, dark tone.

For a moment, I feel a little bad for the guy. He really has no options that benefit him here, but he also came to our house to kidnap me, or "have fun" as he put it. When he said that, I thought he meant rape, which sent a shiver down my spine, but then he mentioned that Marko said I'm to be untouched.

I don't know, but the leader of the FC seems a little unhinged. I have no idea how we are going to stop him, unless we get him put behind bars.

That is the only legal option, anyway.

Decker turns around and looks at me, then pulls me to the side so Ryder can't hear. "Cara, what would you like to do? This is about you, and you should have your say."

"I think we need to get Marko locked up," I say. "That's the only way this is going to end. Well, that, or he dies."

Decker's eyes widen at my bloodthirsty comment. "I agree. What do we do with this guy, though?"

Felix reappears and takes Clover aside. I'm curious what they are talking about, but Decker's question pulls me back to Ryder.

"I know Felix will want to take him in. Can he charge him with breaking and entering?"

Decker shakes his head. "We won't be able to show the security footage because that would show Atlas grabbing him and dragging him inside."

"Felix just went to check the security footage of the car they came here in—Ryder's driving without a license plate and a car of that description was reported stolen. Felix will take him in for that and he won't have to mention the breaking and entering," Clover says.

"Perfect," Decker agrees, cupping my cheek with his palm. "How are you holding up?"

"I'm fine, I just want this over with to be honest," I admit, leaning into his hand.

"You and me both."

Decker, Clover and Atlas come over and we all huddle into a group to decide Ryder's fate. "Who votes to lock him up?" I ask.

Everyone agrees.

"I think it's the best option. Hurting him might backfire," Atlas says, nodding. "And Marko's mental health is clearly hanging on by a thread."

"All right, I'll take him in," Felix agrees. "But we need a proper plan. Marko has a shitload of minions that he can keep sending here. Sure, we could lock them all up but it's going to be a long process."

"I agree," I say, sharing a look with Clo. "We need a solid plan."

Felix arrests Ryder and takes him into the station. Decker goes to check the perimeter, while we order in some food for us all. Clover calls me over, and we sit down with Atlas.

"So I've been picking Atlas's brain, and I think I've come up with a plan," she announces, drumming her fingers on her knee. She puts her hand up. "Before you ask, no, it's not a great plan, and Decker and Felix are going to hate it."

"Why do you say that?" I ask, my tone wary.

Atlas smirks. "Because the two of you are going to be bait."

"I can't just sit around and let them come after my best friend!" Clover yells at Felix, hands on her hips.

The second we told Decker and Felix about Clover's plan, it started a huge fight, and both of them have said that there is no way in hell that they are going to put us in harm's way.

"This plan isn't going to happen," Decker says from beside me, and not for the first time. "We will come up with a better plan, one that doesn't use the two of you as bait. What kind of men do you think we are?"

"We aren't just sitting around," Felix says, shaking his head. "Clo, you aren't doing this."

I have to admit that Clover's plan is pretty damn risky. She wants us to let ourselves get caught by the FC, have a tracker and a microphone on us, then to let Felix and his police team come rescue us. They would arrest Marko and whoever else is there at the time. It would take all of the FC down, and it would be enough to lock them away for a long time.

"Tell me another way then," she says, hands in the air all dramatically. "Tell me a faster way we can get these guys behind bars where they belong. Tell me. I'll wait."

Felix opens his mouth, then closes it. "Decker and I can—"

"They don't want you two, they aren't going to take

you in," she cuts him off. "They want Cara! And if I'm there, I'm sure they will take me, too."

"And if they don't?" he fires back. "You're going to let Cara go in there by herself? What do you think could happen to her?"

"I'm betting that she won't be going alone, but if she does, Cara is a lot stronger than you all give her credit for. She may be a teacher, but she's just as badass as the rest of us. And she won't be in there long before we come and save her. And you heard Ryder—there was a callout for her to remain untouched."

"Nope," Decker says, shaking his head. He turns to me. "I might not be your official man yet, or whatever, but no fucking way in hell am I allowing this to happen. I'm not sending the woman I could potentially marry one day into a fucking gang member's house. It's just not happening."

We all go silent.

"What did you just say?" I whisper, not sure that I heard him correctly.

He scrubs his hand down his face. "I'm just saying. You could be the one. Fuck, it's the opposite of the plan and it hasn't even been that long—"

I cut off his rant with a deep kiss, straddling him. I ignore Clover clearing her throat and Felix chuckling.

I pull back and look into those green eyes. "That was cute, Decker."

I know it sounds crazy, and there was that whole thing with the timing. But I don't want to miss out on this wonderful man just because society tells me I need to be alone for a certain amount of time before diving into something new.

He sighs, lip twitching. "Well then."

We rest our foreheads against each other, just enjoying the moment.

Decker smiles, and it hits me right in the chest.

"Guess we better keep you safe," he whispers, kissing me again.

Yeah, I guess we better.

Chapter Twenty-Nine

Decker

I've never mentioned the word *marry* to a woman before. But I did mean it.

They say that when you know, you know.

And I *know*.

I have a good feeling about her, about us. I know we have a lot more getting to know each other, and plenty to learn about each other, but I'm here for it.

"Never thought I'd see the day that Seth Decker admits he has genuine feelings for a woman," Felix says to me the second we are alone. "Marry. I wish I had recorded that, because no one would believe me if I told them."

"See, I wasn't scared of commitment. I was just waiting for the right woman to come along."

"Yes, well, you better not break her heart or my wife will murder you with her bare hands," he casually warns me.

"Oh, I believe it," I mutter.

The two of them have a friendship that I've never seen between two people before. There's no jealousy, just pure love and support. They'd die for each other, without even thinking about it.

And I love that Cara has that.

I've read about women calling their best friends their soul mates, and I feel like that sums them up.

But that doesn't mean there's not room for me.

"I have to admit, you threw the M word out at the right time. Now they're talking about it instead of them wanting to walk right into Marko's fucking house, or wherever gangs congregate these days. I think it was a brilliant distraction. What are we going to do?"

"Atlas said they have a warehouse they use as their base," I say, sighing. "And yeah, I agree. That plan of theirs is not fucking happening. I'm not opposed to locking them up somewhere if they try it. We need another plan, though, or they aren't going to let it go."

"Yeah, and they'll say that we're trying to control them. I know how this works. We become the bad guys for wanting them to stay safe, like it's a crime," he says, a little too passionately, like this isn't his first time dealing with this.

And with Clover as his wife, I bet it's not.

"I think I know what we need to do," I say, quieting my tone. "We need Rhett to get his ass back here, because he's the one they really want. What better bait than Rhett himself? There's no way that Cara should have to be put in danger because of what he did."

"You just told her you see yourself ending up with her and now you want to bring her ex back into the fold? I've said this before and I'll say it again: you have some big fucking balls, Decker," Felix whisper-yells, looking both shocked and amused.

"Well, this is the only way I can think of to keep her safe. She said that she doesn't love him anymore, so I don't have anything to worry about, right?"

"Yeah, nothing except a shitload of history. And years of close love and friendship," he mutters under his breath.

For a second, I reconsider my idea, but no, this is what Cara needs to be safe. And I'll have to deal with whatever comes with that. I know what we have together.

It's something.

"How are you going to find him?" Felix asks, brow furrowing.

"I'm going to get you to get Clover in on it, and then I'll go to wherever he is and bring him back," I explain. "Or if we can I'll call his ass and tell him to come back. If he has any honor, and I have heard that he does, he won't want Cara and Clover in danger. He will come back and accept his fate."

"Death?"

"Well, if it's him or Cara, guess who I'm choosing?"

"What are you two whispering about?" Clover asks nosily as she steps into the kitchen, eying us both.

"Where's Cara?" I ask, deflecting.

"She's chatting with Atlas. Why?"

"We have a plan, but we need your help. It will protect both you and Cara," Felix says, wrapping her in his arms. "I know you don't like not telling Cara things, but if this works out, we can all be back to normal. Cara will be safe, and Sapphire can come home."

Well played, bringing up their daughter.

Clover hesitates. "I do miss her. What do you both have in mind?"

"Do you know how to contact Rhett?" I ask, keeping my voice low. "He is going to return and he is going to be the bait, not you and Cara. Same plan—we get Marko and his crew arrested, but don't you think Rhett would want to come and face this instead of getting women to do it for him?"

Clover winces, and I'm sure that she knows I'm right. Any man who is worth anything wouldn't want women taking the heat for him. "He called Cara from a burner phone, and she told him we were safe so he didn't come here and get himself killed," she says.

I'm not going to lie; it hurts. Cara didn't tell me Rhett called her, for one, but also she's still trying to protect him, even though it's putting us all in danger.

"But I could probably get his number from Mom," Clover agrees after a few moments. "I'll call her now. Cara is going to hate us going behind her back, though."

"Yeah, but she'll be alive to hate us."

Clover nods slowly and heads to her bedroom to speak with Faye.

"You sure we're doing the right thing here? The Wind Dragons sent him away for a reason," Felix says quietly.

"And what is their reason?" I ask, needing to understand.

"From what I've gathered, Rhett is going to be their president one day. They need him alive," Felix admits. "And with all of us down here, it looks like we have it all under control."

They need him alive, but it's at our expense.

"Why do we"—I motion to Felix and myself—"along with the Knights, need to fight Rhett's battle here? Why are we the ones being put in danger? Give me one reason and I'll back off."

Felix just looks at me. He knows I'm right.

I can't control what others do. I can only try to keep those that I care about safe.

They might be loyal to Rhett.

But I am not.

Chapter Thirty

Cara

Decker says he has to go and take care of some work, and I tell him to be careful. I'd never be able to live with myself if something happened to him because of me.

Con calls me and we have a long chat. I feel so bad that I haven't been able to see her or get to know her properly because of this whole situation. I promise her that we will catch up soon. I know she thinks I'm just ignoring her and maybe don't want to get to know her, but that's not it at all.

I call Natalie next, missing my sister. "How are you?" she asks.

"Fine. I'm stuck inside, just trying to stay alive, you know how it is."

"Don't even joke," she grumbles. "I'm doing the same. I had to miss two of my exams. Luckily they are going to let me retake them, but still. I have to come up with a doctor's note, so now I'm going to have to bribe a doctor or something."

"I'm sorry," I say. "But you will still get to do them,

and you will ace them, like always. I'm just happy to know that you are safe."

"We are fine. We're just worried about you. Dad wanted to come down with a few of the men, but then it leaves us without protection, and the Knights have said they will handle it. Dad's not happy. He literally walks around the clubhouse all day, pacing, like a fucking zombie."

"Tell him I'm fine. I'm living with an FBI agent, a cop and an ex-cop. I think I'm good."

Natalie laughs. "True. And a sexy ex-cop at that. Mom said the sparks were literally flying off from you two."

"I like him," I admit.

"And I like seeing you happy, big sister. You deserve it."

I'm smiling when we end the call, and Clover comes and sits next to me. "Where did Decker go?"

"To his office, I think."

She hesitates, and gently nudges me with her arm. "I don't think the men liked our plan."

"They didn't seem to, no."

"They think that they have a better one," she grumbles, wrapping her arm around me. "You know I love you, right?"

I still. "What did you do, Clover?" I know my best friend well enough to know when she is being sketchy. We don't like to lie to each other, and there have been times, like now, when I can tell that she has done something or knows something I'm not going to like.

"You trust me, right?"

"Of course I do—"

"Okay, well, then—"

She's cut off when Felix rushes into the room. "We have a problem."

"What?" Clover and I both ask in unison. We both stand up, alert, bracing ourselves for what the fuck else has gone wrong now.

"Apparently Con just came to the house to drop off some flowers for you, Cara," he says, scrubbing his hand down his face. "And they saw her. You know how she kind of looks like you, right?"

"Is she okay?" I ask, grabbing on to Clover's hand and squeezing it.

"Atlas saw a car following hers when she left. So he got into his car and went behind them."

"Fucking hell. I literally just spoke to her and said we would catch up when I could see her." I groan, looking at Clover. "What do we do? I can't just let her be followed by a gang just because she resembles me a little."

"Atlas has it under control for now," Felix assures me, turning me to face him and holding on to my arms. "I'm going to call Decker now. She will be okay."

Felix goes to call Decker, and I start pacing, just like Natalie said our dad was. "If something happens to her because of me—"

"It won't," Clover promises, hugging me. "I hate sitting here and just waiting as much as you do. But us rushing out now isn't the best idea—it could get us all killed."

"Decker is on his way there now," Felix says, a muscle ticking in his jaw. I know he wants to be out in the action, too.

"Clover and I will be fine here, we can hold down the fort. You go and help Decker," I tell him.

He shakes his head. "They have eyes on this place—I don't want to risk it. And yes, I know you both are bad-ass, strong women, but they have numbers. I'm aware you can both defend yourself, but what if, say, ten of them make it through the gates somehow. Then what?"

"The chances of getting through the gates are low—"

"They could still shoot through them like they did last time," he points out.

"I just feel so helpless. I don't want to be sitting here while everyone else is out fighting my fight!"

"You mean Rhett's fight," Felix replies, eyes gentling when our gazes connect. "This isn't your fight, Cara. You've just been dragged into this and used as a scapegoat."

And that is the truth of the situation, but it hurts to hear him say it out like that. This isn't my fight, and none of us should be fighting it. Rhett should be here, sorting his own shit out, but it's all fallen on us.

"It's part of being involved with the club."

"I know," Felix replies gently. "But you aren't *in* the club. Besides, they aren't targeting the rest of the club. Right now they just want to hurt Rhett and they're going to use you to do that."

"Rhett isn't here—"

"Exactly."

I look at Clover, who has her arms crossed over her chest, lost in thought. When she doesn't come to Rhett's defense, I know she feels the same way too, like Rhett should be here solving the whole thing instead of off on a damn vacation while we are getting shot at.

None of us want him hurt, but we didn't exactly ask for any of this either, and now Con has been dragged into it, too.

Fuck.

What a mess.

One minute I was a high school teacher keeping a low profile, and now I'm here, hiding from a gang of forgotten, basically unloved children—or at least that's what I'm getting from their name—and trying to keep everyone I love from being killed.

How did we get here?

"Let's all go then. If they have eyes on us, they will follow us and maybe we can lead them away from Con. We can redirect them," I suggest, grabbing my handbag with my gun in it. "We can all be fucking bait."

Felix and Clover share a look, and I know they are probably wondering if I've finally lost my mind. Maybe I have. All I know is that I'm done sitting here.

"What if we go, and then they chase us, and catch us? Then what?" Felix asks me, brow furrowing. "They shoot us? We shoot them?"

Clover goes into her bedroom and comes out with her gun and a set of keys. Felix looks at her like she has also lost her damn mind.

"What?" she asks, examining her weapon. "I want to be ready just in case we go rogue."

"We are not going rogue. Are you all forgetting I'm a police officer?"

"Exactly," Clover replies, grinning evilly. "You can call for backup if you need. It's perfect. We could make sure Con, Atlas and Decker are safe. Cara is right—we can't just sit here. We need to be where the action is."

Felix's phone rings and he picks it up once he sees it's Decker calling him. "What's up?" He looks over at me and nods. "All right, we will be right there." He pauses, and then says, "Yes, 'we' because you try to tell these two that they're not coming."

Another sigh, and then he ends the call. "Decker wants *me* to go and meet with them. The FC ran Con off the road, but don't worry, she's fine. Decker and Atlas rushed in and shot at the car, so the men drove off. She is going to need a new car, though."

I close my eyes in relief, and then open them, ready to go and see her. "All right, let's go then."

When we arrive at the location, I can see her car crashed into a tree. Felix is right, she's definitely going to need a new one, but I can make sure that is taken care of for her. Decker, Con and Atlas are all standing, leaning against Decker's car, waiting for us.

As soon as the car stops, I jump out and run to Con. "Oh my God, Con. I'm so sorry—are you okay?"

She nods, hugging me. "I'm fine, Cara. I mean, I wasn't expecting to be chased down and run off the road today, but I didn't get hurt. Just a little…shaken, I guess."

"Understandably. This is why I told you I couldn't see you."

She winces, rubbing the back of her neck. "Yeah, I thought you meant, busy with work or family issues. I didn't realize you meant busy trying to stay alive."

"To be fair, this *is* a family problem," Clover says as she walks over and hears our conversation.

I turn to Decker and give him a hug, ignoring his

disapproving look. "Thank you for keeping her safe. You too, Atlas."

"It was kind of fun," Atlas says with a smirk, sharing a look with Decker. "Been a long time since I've been in a car chase. I can see why you all chose to be cops."

"Change of career?" I tease.

He laughs, and shakes his head. "Fuck no. As if they'd take me now."

I look back up at Decker. "What now?"

"Now we get Con home, and get the hell out of here before the FC comes back with more men," he says, tucking my hair back behind my ear. He kisses my forehead. "CJ called Atlas and told him that Marko might agree to a sit-down meeting."

I still. "So he's willing to come up with an agreement to let this all go?"

"I don't think it will be that easy. He's going to want his revenge somehow, but maybe we can think of a way to get him to back off. Maybe the Wind Dragons and the Knights could roll up together or something. You all have power, too, and I think it's time we went on the offensive instead of playing defense."

We drop Con home, and then head back to Clover's. I keep thinking about Decker's words. Maybe he's right. Maybe instead of trying to keep the peace we need to show our power.

Maybe we need to fight.

Chapter Thirty-One

Decker

"Yeah?" Rhett answers his phone with a terse voice.

"Rhett? This is Seth Decker. And we need to talk about Cara." I don't like that I have to make this call, and I hate that I had to use Cara's phone without her knowledge to do so.

"Is she okay?" The mention of her name has him dropping his tough guy image.

"I don't know how much you know or what they're keeping from you, but the FC have been targeting her since you're MIA. And now she's in danger because of you." There's an edge to my voice that I can't help. I know being confrontational isn't the smartest way to get through to him, but this whole situation annoys me.

"What the fuck are you talking about?" he barks out.

So he didn't know. Which is a relief, because if he did, that would make him a pathetic excuse for a man.

I give him a quick rundown on what's happened so far, and he mutters a curse at the end of it. "Fucking hell, I had no idea. I'm packing my bag now and coming back. Tell her I'll be there soon and I'll take care of her and keep her safe," he says.

He thanks me like she's still his, but he has no need to.

She's mine to protect now.

"She's already safe. I'm telling you this so you can get back here and clean up your mess. She doesn't even know that I'm calling you."

"Look, man, Cara and I have a history that you'll never be able to compete with, no matter what you think."

I grit my teeth at his words, but make sure to keep my voice even.

"Okay, well, I'm just going to come out and say it: She loves me. I love her. We're together. So yeah, you may have history, but that's exactly what it is. In the past."

He's quiet for a moment. "We'll see about that," he says, and then hangs up.

Cara might be mad at me for going behind her back and contacting him, but I'm not about to let her get hurt because of him. He needs to man up and clean up this colossal mess he has made before Cara gets hurt.

I don't care if he's the future of the Wind Dragons. Cara is *my* future.

"Do you think they will find out where Con lives?" Cara asks me later that morning, pacing up and down the kitchen. "I don't know if bringing her here would be safer or more dangerous for her."

"I don't know either," I admit, stopping her in her tracks and taking her hand. She comes to stand in between my legs, and I look into her gorgeous eyes. "It's going to be okay. You know that, right?"

"Con could have gotten hurt today."

"But she didn't," I say, leaning forward and kissing her nose. "If you want to bring her here, you can; it's up to you. But I think they just thought she was you, to be honest. She just needs to stay away from us until this is all over."

"We don't even look that much alike," she grumbles.

"You look a little alike," I say with a smile. "I might be biased, but of course I think you are much more beautiful."

She rolls her eyes. "Decker—"

"Yes?"

She cuddles into me, arms wrapped tightly around me. "Thank you for being here."

"You don't need to thank me, Cara. I'm where I want to be."

"Stop being cute," she whispers, pulling back and kissing me softly. Her hands rest on the side of my neck, her breasts pressed up against me.

I do mean it.

I *am* right where I want to be.

Even being chased by gang members, I want to be by her side.

I've never felt this way about a woman before. I've always enjoyed them and loved being around them, but I was never emotionally attached to any of them. I could take or leave them—it wouldn't have bothered me either way, as fucked up as that is.

It's a whole different world with Cara.

And I'm happy to be here.

It's been a while since I've had something to lose, and although it's scary, it's also set my soul on fire.

Clover walks into the kitchen and wraps her arms

around the two of us in a group hug. "Are we celebrating another day of breathing?"

"Something like that," Cara replies, and I can hear the smile in her voice.

Clover lets go of us, pulls out a stool and sits next to me. "What do you think about the Marko meet-up?"

"It's obviously a setup," I comment.

"Yeah, but if we show up with all of our people, what can they do?" Clover replies, leaning her arms back against the kitchen countertop. "We can't keep living like this. I think we just need to meet this guy and either come to an agreement or get him arrested. Those are our two options. I mean, there is a third, but it would probably mean one of us would end up in prison. And Uncle Arrow told me all about prison—it doesn't sound like somewhere I'd like to go."

"Your mom would get you out somehow," Cara reminds her.

Clover shrugs, nodding. "Also true."

"Let me guess, we say we are meeting him one on one. Meanwhile, all of his people and ours are there waiting to come out into the action?"

"Exactly," Felix says. "Except he wants Cara to be the one to meet him so they can talk."

"No fucking way." I shut that down instantly. "Cara has nothing to do with what happened."

"Yeah, but he's fixated on her."

"Exactly why she won't be going," I say through clenched teeth.

"Then who else is going to go?" Cara asks, scowling. "Decker, it has to be me. I appreciate you trying to protect me—in fact, it's pretty damn sexy—but I need to do this. This is how it ends."

"How does it end?" I ask, frowning. "With you getting your way by following your original plan of being the bait?"

"Yes." She smirks.

"We can play this to our advantage," Felix says, slapping me on the back. "I'll tell Atlas we will meet this Marko."

When the girls leave, Felix continues our conversation. "Let the women think that Cara is going to meet Marko, but really we can send Rhett in when he gets here. When did he say he would be back? Tomorrow?"

I nod, feeling uneasy. Is it because of the meet, or because Rhett is returning? Most likely it's both. Rhett returning is going to save Cara, but if something happens to him, I know how upset Cara is going to be.

Do I think Rhett will want Cara back? He'd be an idiot not to, but I can't worry about that right now. As long as she doesn't want to be with him, I don't give a fuck what he wants.

"Let's just see how this plays out," Felix murmurs, as the girls reenter the room.

"Okay," I agree.

But Cara is not walking in to meet Marko alone.

I spend the night making love to her, and when morning comes I feel sick in my stomach. I'm not going to let anything happen to her, but there's always a chance that something can go wrong.

"You okay?" she asks as she exits the bathroom, a white fluffy towel wrapped around her. Her hair is still a little wet, dripping down her shoulders, her cheeks flushed from the hot water and steam.

I want to tell her that I love her, just in case, but I don't.

I'll tell her when this is all over.

"Yeah, you look beautiful."

She smiles widely, removes the towel and uses it to dry her hair, the sunlight from the window hitting her perfect body. "It's all going to be fine. It's going to take a lot more than a street gang with mommy issues to take us all down."

My lip twitches. "I know. If anything goes down, you get the hell out of there, though, all right?"

She doesn't reply, and we both know she wouldn't leave anyone behind to save herself. Instead she bends forward to kiss me. "I'm going to be okay. And then we can go back to our normal lives, whatever the hell that may be. I'll get a job at a school around here, you can go back to work and we can live our lives together. How does that sound?"

"Pretty fucking good," I admit. She smiles, then continues to get ready.

"You know I'll do whatever I have to do to protect you, right?" I warn her, trying to keep my tone light.

"I wouldn't expect any less from you, Decker," she replies, amusement in her tone.

She isn't going to be amused when she finds out what I have planned, but I'm going to have to do the whole asking for forgiveness instead of permission thing.

And pray that she can forgive me.

When I can't sleep later that evening, I head into work, running into Nadia when I get there.

"What are you doing here?" I ask, glancing at my watch. "It's late."

"I could ask the same about you." She smirks, lifting her eyes from her laptop. "I just wanted to tie up some loose ends and now was the only time I could come in. Why are you here? How is Cara?"

"She's fine." I left her in bed, just needing to clear my head a little. And something keeps bothering me about our plan. I don't like it. I don't like that I haven't told Cara about Rhett, and I don't like that our plan is essentially to go there and somehow survive. I need it to be better. And I need to be honest with Cara no matter how angry she gets at me.

I sit down and open my laptop. "I'm glad you're here. I need to find out all the dirt I can on this guy. It's a life-or-death kind of situation."

Nadia's eyes light up with excitement. "Give me his name; I'll help you."

We sit there for over three hours, searching leads, aliases and family trees, but at the end of it, it was well worth it, because I find exactly what I wanted to find.

Dirt on Marko.

I can use this information against him if things don't work out the way I want them to. As it turns out, it's clear the man only cares about himself, not the gang that he has raised to be loyal to him.

My phone rings and Cara's name pops up. "Hey."

"Hey. Where are you?" she asks. "Everything okay?"

"Yeah, I'm still at the office. I'll be home soon."

Home.

It's nice to be able to say that to her.

"Okay," she says softly. "See you soon."

It's in this moment I know that I need to tell her everything, and I do exactly that as soon as I get back to her. We both sit on my couch, and I open up about it all.

"So you went behind my back to contact Rhett, and told him to come here and face Marko so I won't have to do it tomorrow," she summarizes, sounding suspiciously calm.

"Yes." I nod. "And I'm sorry I didn't tell you until now, but I'm not sorry I put that plan into action. I'm not going to let you take the fall for your ex's bullshit and—"

She covers my lips with her finger, stopping me from speaking. "I knew what was happening. And I was waiting for you to tell me."

I still. "You knew I spoke to Rhett?"

She arches her brow and leans back on the bed. "You really thought Clo wouldn't tell me? She's my best friend. We tell each other *everything.*"

"And what? You were testing me to see if I'd be honest?"

She shrugs. "Call it what you will. I know you have my best interests at heart, so I wasn't angry, but we need to be able to tell each other things and trust each other. So yeah, I wanted to see if you would tell me or not."

It was a test.

And lucky for me, I somewhat passed.

"And you aren't angry that he's coming back?" I press.

"I don't want anything to happen to him, but you're right, this is his mess. He should be here to help clean it up. I don't want them to kill him, though, and I'm worried that is what will happen if he's here."

Suddenly Cara's phone rings, and it's her dad. "Hello? Yeah, hold on I'll put you on speaker phone."

"We were able to strike a deal," he explains, and Cara and I share a look.

"What's the deal?" I ask.

"Because his kid recovered from the bullet wound and is fine now, the Wind Dragons argued that Rhett shouldn't have to die," Rake explains. "However, retribution is needed, so Rhett is going to have to fight Marko one on one. He just wants to get a few punches in, I think, to save face."

"He couldn't let the gang see him not have any kind of revenge after what happened."

"Exactly," Rake murmurs.

"That's a pretty good outcome," I think out loud.

"We think so, too."

We say bye and Cara tells her dad she loves him as we end the call.

So we have a new plan: Rhett doesn't die, but gets knocked around a little, and Cara will be safe.

We all will be.

"Hopefully after they fight it out things will slowly go back to normal. I can find a place of my own, and we can go back to the cute dating stage," Cara says.

I laugh and press my lips against her neck. "I'll try to drag the honeymoon stage out with you as long as possible."

She laughs and arches her neck for me.

And I just hope that she knows that I mean it.

I'm never going to get impatient with her, or take her for granted. I'm never going to put her anything but first.

She's mine.

Chapter Thirty-Two

Cara

Decker, Clover, Felix and I pull up in two cars to the meeting place, which is at an abandoned warehouse. The FC must know this place, which gives them the upper hand, but at least it's not where anyone else can get hurt. That's what got us all into this huge mess in the first place.

We brought two cars just in case shit goes south and we have to get on out of here. But I'm hoping Marko keeps to his word and this truly just is a one-on-one fight.

A third car pulls up next to us, windows tinted. I know who is in there, and it's going to be a little awkward to see him, like it would be with any ex. My new man is right next to me, and I know that's going to hurt Rhett, whether he deserves my empathy or not.

I still care about him, and I always will.

Rhett opens the door and gets out. He's wearing jeans and a white T-shirt, with black circles under his eyes, blond hair slicked back.

"Decker—" I start to say.

Rhett opens my door, interrupting me, and flashes me a small smile. "Hello, Cara."

"Hey, Rhett. You look like shit," I blurt out, unable to help myself.

"I've missed you too," he says with a laugh, before I get out of the car. I stand next to him as Decker, Clover and Felix join us.

Rhett opens his arms to me, and I fall into them for a moment, before pulling away. I can feel Rhett's eyes on me, and I can feel beautiful green ones on my back. I don't know what to do to make them both happy, and to let them know that I do care about both of their feelings, so I'm a little awkward with my interaction.

"You're all good?" he asks, and I nod.

"You?"

He shrugs. "I look how I feel."

He then shakes Felix's hand, and then Decker's, their eyes catching and holding for a few seconds. Their handshake looks like they are both squeezing for dominance, and I want to tell them both that we don't have time for this shit right now.

Rhett smiles at Clo next, then wraps his arms around her. "I'm sorry you guys have had to deal with this, but I'm here now."

Clover glances around. "No backup?"

"They're coming," Rhett replies, glancing toward the warehouse. "Let's hope he keeps his word and we all don't end up in a big brawl."

Felix and Decker start discussing something and Rhett pulls me aside quickly to have a chat.

"We need to talk." He looks angry, and I'm not used to seeing that look from him.

"What?" I ask.

"I can't believe you," he murmurs, shaking his head and looking behind me at Decker. "We haven't even been broken up a month and you're already in love with someone else? Was our whole relationship just meaningless to you? I feel like I don't even know you anymore."

"Rhett—"

"Look me in the eye and tell me that you don't love me, Cara," he demands, looking straight at me. He cups my chin with his fingers and leans in closer. I move away, because Decker is in my line of sight and I can see his eyes on us. I don't want him to see Rhett touching me. "I bet you can't."

"Do we have to have this conversation right now?" I ask him, glancing toward the warehouse.

"Yes, we do. I do," he replies, and I know he's not going to let it go,

I don't know how to explain this to him without hurting him, which is the last thing I want to do. But if I want to be with Decker peacefully, I need Rhett to understand we are over. I should've done it the last time we had this talk, but I was confused then. I shouldn't have told him that what is meant to be will be. I need to tell him the truth: that we're never getting back together.

Cue Taylor Swift.

"I'll always love you," I say, keeping my tone gentle. "But I'm not in love with you anymore, and I haven't been for a long time. And you know this. You don't love me like that either, Rhett. Like a friend, but not like a lover. You wouldn't have cheated on me if you loved me like that. And I deserve that love. We know each other so well; we have so much history and so much love for each other. You are my first love, but we aren't meant to be together. Not now. Not ever again."

He squeezes my chin gently and then lets go, leaning back with a grimace. "If I don't love you like that, then why does seeing you move on hurt so much?"

"Because we always thought we'd end up together?" I guess, resting my head on his shoulder. "I know that I always thought you'd be the only one for me. But things change, people change. We grew apart, and there's nothing wrong with that."

"When I was away, I knew I had fucked up and I wanted to make things right with you," he admits quietly. "I guess I don't know how you are letting us go so easily. Why aren't you fighting?"

"Because I was fighting for months that we were together. I knew we lost the fight a long time ago. I was fighting, and it was draining, Rhett. I shouldn't have to fight so hard to be with the man I'm meant to be with."

He closes his eyes for a second before reopening them. "I will always love you."

"And I you."

But Rhett will always love the club more.

And I've found what I've always wanted in the form of a six-foot-four, green-eyed, smartass ex-cop.

"We're ready," Clover calls out. I walk away from Rhett and rejoin the group. I look at Decker but he avoids my eyes.

"We are being watched," Clo says, taking my hand in hers.

True enough, there are two men now standing at the entrance, watching and waiting. Rhett looks down at me. "Stay here."

I shake my head. "No, you aren't going in alone. Imagine what he would do if there was no one to report back to the MC."

"We're all going in together," Felix murmurs, sharing a look with his wife. "Please, Clo, do not go rogue on me right now."

Clover pats her gun holster. "Don't worry, husband. We're all coming out of this alive."

"I'm guessing you don't want to wait in the car," Decker says to me, softly, so no one else can hear. I want to talk to him about what just happened, but it's going to have to wait.

"I think you know the answer to that," I reply. "I'm just as capable, Decker."

"I know, but to me, you are more valuable."

Softening, I reach out to touch his arm. "Like Clo said, we're all coming out of this alive."

I look up to see Rhett watching us both, a look of sadness flashing in his eyes. He clears his throat and looks away. I don't like seeing him look like that. It hurts me, too. But we don't have time for this right now. We need to make sure we are all safe, and we need Rhett to fight Marko to do so.

"All right then, let's do this."

We all walk in together.

The two men escort us silently to where Marko is sitting in the middle of the warehouse, very dramatically, like a king on a throne, except he's on an old, worn chair.

Very fitting.

The warehouse is big, an empty bar, his chair and a boxing ring in the corner.

Marko looks nothing like I had expected. He's maybe in his midthirties, but handsome, with dark hair and dark eyes. He has a glint in his eyes, though, that lets me know he is not a good person. My gut instinct would be to stay away from him.

"Rhett," Marko says, glancing around at all of us. His eyes land on me. "Cara, nice to see you in the flesh."

"You mean when you aren't sending your henchmen to try to kidnap me?" I reply, narrowing my eyes.

"Exactly," he replies, unbothered by my attitude. "But that's all in the past now, isn't it? I struck a deal with the Wind Dragons and the Knights of Fury presidents. Rhett and I will fight, and then it's settled. There will be no more war between us all."

"Just like that it's over?" Rhett asks, pulling off his black hoodie and throwing it on the floor. "That's the deal, right?"

Marko nods and stands. "That's the deal."

What's the catch?

Why does it feel like there's something that we are missing here?

Marko points to the makeshift boxing ring in the corner of the open space. "I'm ready when you are."

All of his men appear from the shadows. There has to be at least fifty of them. They are definitely going to try to use intimidation as a tactic, and with only five of us—I have to admit that it's working on me, anyway.

We told the Wind Dragons and the Knights of Fury to be here as our backup, we were hoping that we wouldn't need them and it wouldn't turn into a huge brawl, but it looks like it's going to be heading that way.

But we're going to have to manage and buy some time until they get here.

Decker puts his arm around me and gently pulls me behind him. We can't trust these people, and we need to be careful with our actions.

"You need your whole gang here to watch you lose?" Rhett asks, and I roll my eyes at his trash talking. I don't know if pushing Marko and all of his followers is the best thing right now. In fact, I know that it isn't.

Hitting his ego in front of all his men?

Bad idea.

"Actually, I want them here to watch me win. To show them what happens when people cross me and my family," Marko fires back, but I can tell that Rhett's comment angered him. This man has a fragile ego, and clearly must be mentally unstable.

Then, as if out of a movie, Marko rips off his white T-shirt, exposing a muscled body, with hair on his chest and a tattoo of a lion covering the side of his torso.

His men all cheer.

I share a look with Decker, and I can see from his eyes that he is as concerned as I am.

"They didn't even check us for weapons," he murmurs, glancing around.

Yeah, he's on edge too.

"What do you think they are going to do?" I whisper.

"I don't know, but if shit goes down, grab Clover and get the fuck out of here," he says, squeezing my hand in a silent plea. "And know that I'm pretty sure you are the one for me."

"You're the one for me, too."

And that's the moment that I fucked up.

Because Rhett hears me say those words, and he turns to me, blue eyes filled with pain.

"Rhett—" I whisper, reaching out for him.

But he turns his back on me.

And then he steps into the ring, pulling his shirt off.

Those words from my lips are the last ones to play in his head before he goes into a fight for his life.

Chapter Thirty-Three

Decker

Rhett stretches his neck from side to side. I watch Cara, and I know this has to be hard for her. Watching the two of them talk privately was hard. What was harder was seeing her mouth the words *I'll always love you* to him, right in front of me. I'm not going to lie, it felt like someone had punched me right in the gut.

I might as well be in that ring too. It would probably be less painful.

"He's going to be fine," I promise her. I turn to Clover, who is clasping on to Felix like a lifeline. "He's a good fighter, right?"

She nods. "Yeah, he's good. Is this definitely a one-on-one fight, though?"

"If it isn't, Marko has called a full-on war with not just the Wind Dragons, but the Knights too. Would he risk that?" Cara asks, sharing a look with Clover. "What's our plan B, guys?"

I mean, we all have guns, but I'm assuming the FC do too. "I have the plan B. I just need the bikers to get here."

I pull my phone out and send a quick text to Temper, telling them to hurry their asses up.

"You ready?" Marko calls out to Rhett, who nods.

Marko then turns to his audience. "These are the rules. We keep fighting until someone gives up, or someone is knocked the fuck out. You can tag in two other people if you need a break, but only two at a time in the ring."

"That wasn't the deal," Clover calls out, stepping forward with her hands on her hips. "The deal was a one-on-one with you and Rhett, and then it was settled."

Marko calls out two of his men, huge motherfuckers that belong on one of those old warrior movies. One must be nearly seven feet tall, and pure muscle. The other is smaller, but no doubt well trained and just as deadly.

"I changed my mind," Marko replies, laughing. "I think this will make it more interesting, don't you think? And it's still fair."

Felix turns to me. "I call shot-gun on not fighting that tall bastard."

Fuck.

Technically, Marko is right, three versus three is still a fair fight, one fighting at a time, but he knew this and brought in these WWE bastards, who could easily destroy most men. He didn't want to just teach Rhett a small lesson; he wanted to set that giant on him to annihilate him.

That was Marko's plan all along, to destroy Rhett— have him broken, beaten and bloody, and then still call it a fair fight.

I personally don't think having one man the size of

the rest of us put together is a fair fight, but this is what we've been given to work with.

And you know what? A big man goes down harder.

Marko doesn't know I'm a martial artist, so he probably would have thought that we would have been easily beaten. Or maybe he does know, but assumes his giant will trump all...

And maybe he will.

But little does he know I don't like to fucking lose.

Especially not when I'm fighting in front of my woman.

I quickly eye all the men, taking in any weak points just by observing their body language and posture.

"Let me fight," I hear Clover tell Felix, and I wince, feeling sorry for Felix. I'm glad Clover isn't my problem.

"Clover, no," I hear Felix reply, his tone full of steel.

I ignore their arguing over who beat who in the police academy and turn to Cara.

"Who is going to fight against that behemoth of a man?" she asks, whisper-yelling. "I have a bad feeling about this."

"We're going to have to fight these assholes."

She purses her lips. "You're going to fight him, aren't you? Decker, don't get me wrong—"

"What choice do we have? I'm the best fighter out of us," I tell her, cupping her cheek in my hand. "And it will be fine. Have a little faith."

"Oh, I have faith in you. But I don't think I've ever even seen a man that size," she replies, staring at said man in concern. "He looks like he could eat me."

"No one other than me will be eating you," I remark in a dry tone.

She flashes me a "this is not the fucking time" look and I can't help but grin.

The fight begins, and we all move closer to the ring. Marko and Rhett both start circling each other, arms up in fighting stance. Rhett is taller than Marko, but as they commence throwing punches, it's quick to see that Marko is indeed a good fighter. But so is Rhett.

"Come on, Rhett!" Clover calls out, encouraging him.

"Both of you stay together," I tell Cara and Clover, and Felix and I get ready for whenever Rhett decides to tag us in. I'm not going to lie, I'm fucking nervous, and I don't know how this is going to play out. If we win, will they just let us walk away? Or will he throw in some other last-minute rules and find a way to make us all pay?

I don't trust Marko, and I don't think that he will let us make him look bad in any way, shape or form.

Rhett lands a good punch to Marko's jaw, and I know that had to hurt. He lets out a growl of anger and tries to lash back at Rhett, who ducks and hits him in the stomach. Marko gets in one good hit, but Rhett hits him back even harder and Marko falls to the ground.

He yells out, "Stalk!"

The giant walks over and steps into the ring. Marko taps his hand, smirking.

Ah fuck, here we go.

Rhett stares up at his new opponent, up and fucking up because he's so tall and wide, but props to Rhett—

he doesn't show any fear or hesitation. He just puts his hands up and gets ready to fight.

"I can't look," I hear Cara whisper, and Clover hugs her tightly.

"We're all going to get our asses kicked today, aren't we?" Felix mutters from beside me.

"None of us knew he had the Hulk as his sidekick. Neither did we know we'd have to fight." I mean, damn, I would have done some better preparation if I knew about it. But we are here now, and we have to do whatever we need to do to get out of here with the women untouched, and all of our limbs still in place.

"Do you think they call him Stalk because he's as tall as a fucking beanstalk?" I hear Clover ask Cara.

Rhett and Stalk start their round in the ring, and I watch his moves. Just like I thought, Stalk might be strong but he's slower than Rhett, and I notice him favoring his right leg instead of his left. I suspect he might have a bad knee, and that's the first spot I'm going to go for when I end up against him.

"Clover, there's no way in hell you are getting in that ring," Felix says, shaking his head. Clover stays quiet, probably realizing that even she is in over her head with this one.

"I won't let her do anything stupid," Cara promises us.

Rhett punches Stalk in the gut, but he doesn't even flinch, like he didn't even feel it.

"What the fuck," Felix groans, then turns to me. "I could call in the cops for backup. Get these fuckers arrested."

"How the hell are we going to explain us being

here?" I ask, keeping my tone low. "And what will we have them arrested for? Nothing that would hold."

"I don't know, but any plan sounds better than fighting that guy."

He's not wrong.

The women cry out, and I turn back to the ring to see Rhett on all fours, blood pouring from his likely broken nose. All it took was one hit to get him to his knees, and I can't imagine how hard that hit would have been.

"We can't let him take another hit," I say.

"I know, but what happens when we go down?" Felix asks.

"I guess we're about to find out," I mutter. I pull off my T-shirt and step into the ring, behind Rhett. "Tag me in."

"No," he replies, spitting out blood. "This is my mess, I finish it."

"You'll die," I say, bending down next to him. "Tag me in, Rhett. Don't be an idiot."

He shakes his head and stands back up, stretching his neck from side to side. He is obviously a stubborn, prideful asshole, and I totally see where he is coming from, but right now, I need to save him from himself. He doesn't need to do this. We might not be friends, but we are on the same side, and Cara cares about him. That means something to me, and I'm not going to allow him to take a damn beating in front of her.

Marko, who obviously wants Rhett to stay in the ring to get the shit kicked out of him, starts to egg him on. "What's wrong, Rhett? Can't handle it? Going to get your ex's new boyfriend to handle shit for you? Maybe she did the right thing by trading up?"

Fucking low blow.

I'm fuming by this point. "Just like you couldn't finish fighting Rhett yourself? You had to have your fucking Hagrid here step in for you. Rhett is more of a man than you will ever be, so shut the fuck up."

There is dead silence for a few moments.

My sister always said that my big mouth was going to get me into trouble one day, and it looks like right now is going to be that time.

Rhett looks over at me in surprise. "What the fuck are you doing? You really think you can fight this guy?" His nose is broken and there's blood covering his chest. I wouldn't be surprised if his ribs were also broken. He's not in good shape, but he's pretending like he's fine.

"I don't know but we're about to find out."

I offer him my hand, and he tags it.

I didn't wake up this morning planning on some WWE shit, but here I am.

Helping save the man that the woman I love also loves.

Chapter Thirty-Four

Cara

"Your man has a death wish," Clover whispers next to me, her eyes as wide as saucers. She's been commentating this whole thing, and I can't deal with her right now. "He has a good body, though. I hope Stalk doesn't rip it up."

I'm going to kill her.

"I know you said he's a good fighter, but I've never even seen him fight," I say to Felix, panicking.

"I'm confused as to what is going on right now. What happens if Decker's nose or something gets broken? You jump in, and then what? I'll have to hold Clover back and then we'll probably get our asses kicked too."

"Decker is going to be fine," Felix says to me. "And no, the two of you won't be getting into the ring. Calm down, Cara, it will be okay. Trust us."

"Okay."

Decker made Rhett come back so I wouldn't take the fall for him, but now Decker's doing that himself. He's helping someone he doesn't even know—or let's be real, like, because who likes someone's ex? He has every reason to hate Rhett and to want to see him get hurt, but he doesn't.

It's clear that Decker has a good heart, and I love that about him, but right now, I'm stressing out.

Felix helps Rhett out of the ring, and I can tell he's hurting and dealing with quite a few broken bones.

"Should we get him out of here?" Clover asks us.

"I don't know if they will let us," Felix replies, nodding to Marko's horde.

"I'm fine," Rhett lies, picking his T-shirt up and using it to stanch the blood from his nose. "Fucking fine."

Decker and Stalk face each other, and Decker throws the first punch, nailing the guy in the stomach. The two of them start moving, and I can see that Decker is, in fact, a pretty badass fighter. He moves quickly and precisely, and although his opponent is much bigger, Decker is faster and more skilled.

He might be able to win this.

"He's good," Clover comments, nodding in appreciation. "I wish Mom was here, she'd love this shit."

Decker lands a strong kick right into Stalk's knee, and he falls down.

Hard.

Decker really knows what he's doing, and not that I'd ever admit it, but I'm low-key turned on by the whole thing.

When I see movement in the corner of my eye, I turn to see the Knights of Fury MC show up, stepping into the warehouse like they own the damn place.

What perfect timing.

"Looks like we're just in time for the show," a man calls out, taking in the scene before him.

"What show is this? Fucking *Game of Thrones*?" a light-haired man asks, staring at Stalk. "He's massive. He should be fighting at least three men at the same time."

"Crow." Another man laughs.

Marko walks over to greet the first man who spoke, which makes me think he must be their president, Temper. "We had a deal, and I'm sticking to that."

"I thought the deal was for you and Rhett to fight and make up. Why is Decker in there fighting a man three times his size?" Temper asks, scowling.

"And he's winning," Crow points out.

Temper is an intimidating man; I can see why no one would want to mess with him. In some ways, he reminds me a little of Uncle Arrow. Speaking of, I smile widely when my dad, Sin, Arrow, Tracker, Vinnie and Talon step inside behind the Knights. Dad's eyes go straight to me, and I can see him sighing in relief.

I know exactly how he feels.

Talon walks over to Rhett, his stepson. "Come on, let's get out of here before any shit goes down."

"We're just here to make sure you stick to your side of the deal, Marko, and that this beef is over," Arrow says, crossing his arms over his chest. "And if it's not, we're here to start another one."

Marko swallows hard. "My son was injured!"

"But he's fine now, and we are happy to pay for the medical bills. Rhett is extremely sorry about what happened," Arrow continues, looking over at Rhett.

"And now he is injured, and he is an MC member's son. Shouldn't that be even?"

Marko nods slowly. "I suppose so."

"Fucking wonderful," Arrow replies, looking to Temper. "You getting your man out of the ring or we letting him fight anyway?"

Temper laughs and looks over at Decker. "My man? He's dating one of yours."

"Don't all fight over me," Decker calls out in a dry tone, stepping out of the ring and coming over to me.

I hold him tightly and say, "You know what? I think you would have won that."

"I think so too," he says, not a humble bone in his body. "But I'm glad I didn't have to. You guys should get the fuck out of here before something else happens."

"We? What about you?" I ask, brow furrowing.

"I want to stay back and make sure this is all over with," he says, kissing me on the forehead. Felix and Decker share some words, and then Felix walks back over and tells us we should go.

"Should I stay with him?" I ask Felix, worried.

"Nah, he's fine," he assures me.

I see Temper head over to speak to Marko privately, and Decker joins them. I wonder what is going on. The Knights and Wind Dragons linger behind with Decker, while we get into our cars and head home.

"What's going on?" I ask Clo as we drive off. "Why is Decker there talking to Marko?"

"I don't know, but I think they have a plan to make sure it's over and that we're safe." She pauses, and then adds, "I think Decker wants to know it's definitely safe for you now. We should go and make sure Rhett is okay. Talon will have taken him back to our house."

Sure enough, Talon and Rhett are sitting in their car, waiting for us to arrive home.

"You didn't go to the hospital?" I ask Rhett when we both drive inside the gate and get out of the car. "You have a broken nose and God knows what else."

"I'm fine," he replies, tone curt.

"I'll call my nurse friend to come here and see him if that's okay, Clo. He refused to be taken to the hospital," Talon explains, not sounding surprised about that fact. He probably does the same thing.

"Yeah, of course," Clover replies, pulling her keys out. "Let's get him inside."

We help Rhett inside and sit him down on the couch. Clover gets him some water, and we both help him clean up his face.

"Yeah, someone is going to have to reset your nose," I mutter.

He looks up at me, silently, for a few seconds before speaking. "He's a good man."

"I know," I whisper. "But so are you."

He laughs, and then flinches. "I don't know, I probably would have left me there to suffer if I were in his shoes."

I roll my eyes and he smiles sadly, and reaches out to touch my face. "As long as you're happy, Cara."

"I am. Now you get happy, too."

This has to be one of the hardest moments of my life. But I need to be honest about what I want, and that happens to be Decker.

I love who I am with him, I love how he treats me, and I love the idea of this new chapter in my life.

Chapter Thirty-Five

Decker

When Cara leaves, I show Arrow and Temper the evidence that Nadia and I found on Marko. Temper smirks, and he knows that we've won with this one.

"Do your gang members know that you were a police informant?" I ask Marko, who goes still. "Or are you still one?" He glances around to see if anyone can hear.

"I don't know what you're talking about," he replies, lifting his chin.

I show him the evidence—testimony court documents. "They might like to see this to show them who they are blindly following."

Who knows when these photos were taken, but they show what type of man Marko is, or Marvin Keen, which is his birth name. As per my plan, I wanted Arrow and Temper here before I showed the evidence. There's now no way for Marko to get out of this.

"They will kill me," he whisper-yells. "What do you want? I will keep my word and leave the fucking Knights and Dragons alone. Whatever you want."

I share a look with the two MC Presidents.

Arrow speaks first. "I want you off my territory." He looks to Temper.

"I want the same. We don't want you anywhere near us. Move your men and get the fuck out of here, or we will tear you down," Temper agrees.

Marko opens his mouth, then closes it, gritting his teeth. "Okay, fine. You will never see us again. But do everything you can to bury that evidence, and it's never to be spoken of again."

We all agree. Arrow and Temper both shake my hands.

"You sure you don't want to join the MC?" Temper asks me as we walk back to my car. "We could use someone like you. Fuck, anyone who is willing to fight a man that size and look like he might actually win would be an asset."

I shake my head. "I appreciate the offer, but no thank you. I'm happy where I'm at right now."

"Offer's always open."

I drive back to Clover's, just processing everything that happened today. All that matters now is that Cara is safe, and we can maybe try getting into a normal routine. I'm looking forward to going back to work, and enjoying getting to know Cara in a less stressful setting.

I step into the house and hear Cara and Rhett having another chat in the living room.

I knew the situation I was getting myself into—that she was fresh from a break up—but knowing that she told him she loves him hurts me more than I thought it ever would. And now they are sitting there alone together, having another private conversation.

I slowly exit, get back in my car and drive home.

Maybe she changed her mind and decided to be with him. Or maybe she loves us both. I don't know if I can deal with that, though.

But at least she's safe now.

I'm just getting out of the shower when I hear a banging at my door. I grab my gun just in case, but put it down when I look out the window and see Cara standing there, her cute face scrunched up in anger.

"What are you doing?" she asks when I open the door. She steps inside and closes it behind her.

"What?"

"Why didn't you come back to Clover's house to see me? I was waiting for you," she asks, shifting on her feet.

"I did come back. You were having a talk with Rhett, so I left you alone so you could have your privacy," I admit, trying to keep my tone even.

"I was having a chat with him, yes, but so what? I was worried about you. I didn't know why you stayed behind."

"So, what? You told him that you love him before we went into the warehouse. That's a little more than a 'so what'," I return, jaw clenching.

Her eyes widen and her face goes from anger to understanding in a second. "Decker—"

She said that to him. We haven't even said that to each other yet, which is fine since it's only been a short time we've been together, but still. If that didn't make me feel put in my place, nothing will.

"I want to be with you, Cara. I'm crazy about you.

I don't care how fucking fast we have moved, or what people think about us. But I need you to feel the same way about me. If you still love Rhett, then what are we doing here?" I ask, my towel accidentally falling to the floor, ruining my whole dramatic speech.

I know that she tries not to look, but her eyes dart south, staring at my cock—which is hard, because of course it is with her in front of me. And yeah, maybe fighting with her makes me horny.

"My eyes are up here," I say in a dry tone.

She steps forward. "I did tell Rhett I love him, and I do. I always will. But not in that way. I'm not in love with him. He will always be special to me as someone I have history with, and someone that I care for. But he's not my future. You are. I told you this, and nothing has changed for me."

"Cara—"

"And you know what? The fact that you *still* protected me, and helped save him even after everything, shows me what kind of man you are."

She reaches out to stroke my cock gently. "Do you think I'm stupid enough to let someone like you go? Someone who protects me, loves me, has the most amazing eyes, and body…" She glances down at me. "You are perfect, Decker. I don't care what anyone thinks either. If you'll have me, I'm yours."

I reach out and grab her, pulling her closer and kissing her. "Of course I fucking want you," I say against her lips. I lift her up and carry her back to my bedroom, throwing her on the black sheets and undressing her.

I don't care if she will always love Rhett.

It shows the type of loving woman that she is.
Mine.
She's mine.
And that's all that there is to it.

Epilogue

Cara holds Sapphire in her arms as she reads her a story, then tucks her into her bed. We came to Clover and Felix's house for dinner, and Cara offered to help Clover with Fire's bedtime routine. There's something about watching a woman with a baby or small child— or maybe it's just Cara, because with any other woman I probably would have run.

But I could see her being the mother of my children. Watching her now makes the caveman side of me want to have her barefoot and pregnant.

"What?" she asks softly, noticing me staring at her.

"You just look good with a baby," I say, licking my lips. "A little too good."

She smirks. "Don't worry, I feel the same way when I watch you with her."

"Good."

We leave the room and head back into the kitchen, where Clover and Felix are whispering shit to each other and laughing.

"Don't mind us," I comment.

Clover turns around and smiles. "As if you two can talk—you are the worst," she replies, pouring us all a glass of red wine. "Now, Cara, tell us all about your new job."

Cara started work at a local high school this week, and she moved straight in with me. I know it's probably not the best idea, but we both don't give a fuck. I wanted to be with her, and she with me, and it's worked out perfectly. I love coming home to her, and she has made my house into a home.

She and Simone get on wonderfully, like I knew that they would, and we've been spending some time getting to know Con, too.

"Well, no one knows about my connection to a motorcycle club, so it's pretty good. No one is scared to talk to me," she says, grinning. "No, but it's actually really nice. The kids are wonderful, and I'm really enjoying it. It's been a nice change."

After the whole incident at the warehouse, Cara's father gave me his blessing. I might not be a Wind Dragon like Rhett, and he might not know me that well, but I would do anything for his daughter, and I think he saw that. He respects me for how I handled everything, and it's nice to have her parents' approval.

I doubt I have Rhett's approval, but he has not shown up at our door starting any shit. He loves Cara enough to let her be happy. I know they still talk and get together with Clover. I respect that friendship.

"Well, I for one am happy that you decided to stay in

town," Clover says, smiling at us all in turn. She lifts her wineglass. "To friendships, new and old."

"To family," Cara adds, and we all clink glasses.

To true love, I think in my head.

The greatest blessing.

* * * * *

Acknowledgments

A big thank-you to Carina Press for working with me on this new series!

Thank you to Kimberly Brower, my amazing agent, for having my back in all things. We make a great team, always have and always will.

Brenda Travers—Thank you so much for all that you do to help promote me. I am so grateful. You go above and beyond and I appreciate you so much.

Tenielle—Baby sister, I don't know where I'd be without you. You are my rock. Thanks for all you do for me and the boys, we all adore you and appreciate you. I might be older, but you inspire me every day. When I grow up, I want to be like you.

Sasha—Baby sister, do you know one of the things that I love about you? You are you. You don't care what anyone else thinks, you stay true to yourself and I am so proud of you. Tahj reminds me of you in that way. Never change. I love you.

Christian—Thank you for always being there for me, and for accepting me just the way I am. Thank you for trying to understand me. We are so different, opposites in every way, but I think that's the balance that we both need. I always tell you how lucky you are to have me in your life, but the truth is I'm pretty damn lucky myself. I appreciate all you do for me and the boys. I love you.

Mum and Dad—Thank you for always being there for me and the boys no matter what. And thank you, Mum, for making reading such an important part of our childhood. I love you both!

Natty—My bestie soul mate, thank you for being you. For knowing me so well, and loving me anyway. I hope Mila sees this book one day and knows her Aunty Chanty loves her so much!

Sasha Jaya & Aunty Starlyn—I love you both so much! You are the meaning of family.

Ari—Thank you for still being there for me, helping me with my website and anything else that pops up. You are one of the best humans I've ever known.

To my three sons, my biggest supporters, thank you for being so understanding, loving and helpful. I'm so proud of the men you are all slowly becoming, and I love you all so very much. I hope that watching me work hard every day and following my dreams inspires you all to do the same. Nothing makes me happier than being your Mama.

And Chookie—No, I love you more.

And to my readers, thank you for loving my words. I hope this book is no exception.

About the Author

New York Times, Amazon and *USA TODAY* bestselling author Chantal Fernando is thirty-four years old and lives in Western Australia.

Lover of all things romance, Chantal is the author of the bestselling books *Dragon's Lair, Maybe This Time* and many more.

When not reading, writing or daydreaming, she can be found enjoying life with her three sons and family.

For more information on books by Chantal Fernando, please visit her website at www.authorchantalfernando.com.

New York Times *bestselling author*
Chantal Fernando brings you Fast & Fury: A sexy
new series fully loaded with intense emotions and
edge-of-your-seat suspense.

Read on for an excerpt from
Custom Built *by Chantal Fernando,*
out from Carina Press!

Chapter One

"I'm sorry, Bronte," Nadia says, shoulders hunching. "You know how much the business has been struggling for months, and now it's barely making enough money for me to cover my own ass, never mind have an employee. I'm so sorry."

"It's okay," I tell her, forcing a smile, even though I feel like crying. I mean, I knew this was coming. I've worked as an assistant for Nadia's private investigator firm for years now, and I know how hard this decision must be for her. We had spoken about it a few months ago, and to be honest I'm surprised she has kept me on for this long.

However, that doesn't mean it doesn't hurt. I need this job, and I don't know what the hell I'm going to do without it. I don't have any other qualifications, and I can't afford to go back to college to finish my teaching degree. And I don't even want to talk about health insurance. Thank God I had my second surgery several months ago. I can't even fathom what I will do if the abnormal cells come back.

I know how bad times are for Nadia, though, with

us getting less and less work with every passing month. I'd spent this week cleaning and rearranging the office because I didn't have much else to do.

I see Nadia more like family than my boss, but I know that she has to do what's best for her. I understand that—it's just going to be a shit time for me right now.

"I'll pack up my things," I say, and swallow hard, looking at my desk. I pick up the picture of me and my dad, both of us smiling, his arms wrapped around me. It was taken last year at Christmas, my red lipstick all over his cheek where I had kissed him. Dad has always been my rock, and I know he'd help me if I need it, but I'm too old to be running to my daddy. I need to sort this all out myself and find a new job as soon as possible, before my savings dry up and put me in deeper shit.

"I'm really sorry," Nadia repeats, her voice cracking.

I put the photo frame down and turn to give her a hug. "It will be fine, it's not the end of the world. I'll find another job, and hopefully business will pick up for you and you can keep this place running."

This might not be what I need right now, a kick when I'm down, already stressed out over my health issues, but you can't control what curveballs life decides to throw you.

No matter what happens, I know I'll be okay. When one door closes, another one opens, right?

I comfort Nadia, I gather my things, and I leave.

I woke up this morning employed and fairly optimistic, and now I'm going home without a job and no idea where my next paycheck is going to come from.

Life can be a bitch sometimes, can't it?

* * *

Just before Christmas isn't the best time to try to find employment. Everyone has already been hired for the season, and no one wants to take on someone they would have to train during the busy festive season. Not surprisingly, my résumé isn't remarkable, and my private investigator skills aren't even going to help me work in a bar or restaurant.

"Have you ever worked in a bar before?" a manager at one of the establishments asks me.

"Well, no, but—"

"I'm sorry," he says, cutting me off. "We need someone with experience."

"I'm a fast learner."

I mean, how hard could it be, right? It's not like I'm a doctor looking for a new job. I can learn to serve drinks and food and wear a smile while doing it. I'm a hard and efficient worker; I just need someone to give me a chance. I didn't finish college because the timing wasn't right for me.

"Come back after the holidays" is all I get in response.

I decide to call up all the private investigator firms in my city, but none of them are hiring either. In the world of easily accessible technology, people are probably handling their own investigating, cutting out the middleman and leaving me jobless. I really hope Nadia will be okay and not have to shut down the firm. The thought saddens me, and I hope there's a way she can stay open and get more clients in the upcoming weeks.

Otherwise she might be here along with me, trying to get any job she can.

My phone rings, "All I Want for Christmas Is You" playing loudly. "Hello?"

"Hey, princess," my dad says, and I can hear the smile in his tone. "I haven't heard from you in a week. Is everything okay?"

I haven't spoken to him since I got fired, because I don't want to admit that I'm currently failing at life. Asking for help has never been my strong point—I prefer to suffer in silence and try to solve all problems on my own. I know I'm going to have to tell him, though; I'm just going to buy myself a little time.

"Everything is fine, Dad," I assure him. "How are you?"

My dad lives about an hour away from my apartment, and we catch up for family dinner every week or so. Besides that, we usually text or chat every day or every other day. I love spending time with him, and I look forward to seeing him. Yes, I'm a daddy's girl.

"I'm good, just busy with work. You know how it is," he says.

Actually, right now I don't.

My dad has always worked hard, and that's where I got my own work ethic from. As soon as I was old enough to get a job, I did. I was never spoiled, and had to work for everything I had. For my first car, he told me he'd match whatever I saved, which taught me how to work for my money, but also allowed him contribute.

Dad now owns a construction business, along with

my uncle Neville, who also owns and runs a farm. Dad mainly does the admin side of things, but he started off as a laborer, so he isn't afraid of hard work.

"I've been thinking about you today, so I thought I'd give you a call."

"When are you free this week?" I ask. Might as well face him, because avoiding him isn't going to help the situation. I can't lie to him, though, so I guess I'm just going to have to tell him what happened in person. Or maybe I should try to secure a new job first.

"Always free for you," he says, voice gentle. "I was actually calling to invite you over on the weekend. I'm having a barbecue, and everyone will be there. Your uncle wants to see you too, so I hope you can make it."

"Okay, message me the details and I'll be there," I reply. "I'm looking forward to it."

We say our byes and I love yous and hang up. Sighing, I glance down at my handful of résumés and lift my chin. Surely there's something for me out there. I'm too old to have no job security, and it annoys me that it has come to this. I should have gone back and finished my degree—then I'd have something to fall back on—but there's no point with the what-ifs now. I just need to find something, anything, and if I don't like it, I can always just stay in that job until I find something better.

"Who knows? In a few weeks I might have to come apply here," I mutter to myself as we pass Toxic, a well-known strip club.

If I didn't think my father would kill me, I might even consider it.

I spend the rest of the day handing out my résumé, smiling and trying to act as charming as can be.

Just hoping the next door to open for me will be a good one.

Don't miss Custom Built *by Chantal Fernando,*
available wherever books are sold.

www.Harlequin.com